DOCTOR WHO
AND THE
CAVE MONSTERS

THE CHANGING FACE OF DOCTOR WHO
The cover illustration and others contained within this book
portray the third DOCTOR WHO whose physical appearance
was altered by the Time Lords when they banished him to
the planet Earth in the Twentieth Century.

DOCTOR WHO
AND THE
CAVE MONSTERS

Based on the BBC television serial *Doctor Who and the
Silurians* by Malcolm Hulke by arrangement with the BBC

MALCOLM HULKE

Introduction by
TERRANCE DICKS

Illustrated by
Chris Achilleos

BOOKS

3 5 7 9 10 8 6 4 2

Published in 2011 by BBC Books, an imprint of Ebury Publishing
A Random House Group Company
First published in 1974 by Universal-Tandem Publishing Co., Ltd.

Novelisation copyright © Malcolm Hulke 1974
Original script © Malcolm Hulke 1970
Illustrations © Chris Achilleos 1974
Introduction © Terrance Dicks 2011
The Changing Face of Doctor Who and About the Author © Justin Richards 2011
Between the Lines © Steve Tribe 2011

The Random House Group Limited Reg. No. 954009

Addresses for companies within the Random House Group can be found at
www.randomhouse.co.uk

A CIP catalogue record for this book is available from the British Library.

ISBN 978 1 849 90194 9

The Random House Group Limited supports The Forest Stewardship Council
(FSC®), the leading international forest certification organisation. Our books
carrying the FSC label are printed on FSC® certified paper. FSC is the only
forest certification scheme endorsed by the leading environmental organisations,
including Greenpeace. Our paper procurement policy can be found at
www.randomhouse.co.uk/environment

Commissioning editor: Albert DePetrillo
Editorial manager: Nicholas Payne
Series consultant: Justin Richards
Project editor: Steve Tribe
Cover design: Lee Binding © Woodlands Books Ltd, 2011
Cover illustration: Chris Achilleos
Production: Rebecca Jones

Printed and bound by CPI Group (UK) Ltd, Croydon, CR0 4YY

To buy books by your favourite authors and register for offers,
visit www.randomhouse.co.uk

Contents

INTRODUCTION
BY
Terrance Dicks

It's a great pleasure to write the introduction to Mac Hulke's 'Cave Monsters' – or to give it its proper title, 'The Silurians'.

(In the early days of the novelisations the first editor, Richard Henwood, would arbitrarily change the titles of stories to something he felt was more saleable. 'Silurians?' he said. 'They'll never understand that! We'll call it "The Cave Monsters".' Later on, as the books gained in sales and status, the practice was quietly dropped.)

I take a particular interest in 'The Silurians', since it was written by my old friend and mentor Mac Hulke. We met, purely by chance, when I took a couple of rooms in the house he owned in Hampstead. We became good friends, and he gave me my start in television when we collaborated on a script for *The Avengers*. It's a tribute to Mac's generosity that he insisted on a joint credit and a fifty-fifty split on the money. Later we wrote three more *Avengers* scripts together.

Mac was, to put it mildly, quite a character. Short, balding and bespectacled, he had a razor-sharp mind and inexhaustible energy, and he was incredibly well organised. Behind a sharp-tongued, often acerbic manner, he was extraordinarily kind and helpful.

It was Mac who recommended me as one of the *Crossroads* writing team, and it was on *Crossroads* that I met Derrick

Sherwin who called me some time later and said, 'How would you like to be Script Editor of *Doctor Who*…'

Before I'd fully taken over from Derrick, he came into my office one day and said, 'Two script projects have collapsed. We need a ten-part *Doctor Who* serial, you've got to write it and we need it next week…'

Naturally I turned to Mac. Together we co-wrote 'The War Games'. Equally naturally, Mac was one of the writers I approached when setting up my first season of *Doctor Who*.

There's another reason for my special interest in 'The Silurians' – I think I can claim that I came up with the original idea. Though, to be fair, the idea was sparked off by a shrewd observation from Mac.

It happened like this. By the time Barry Letts and I took over as Producer and Script Editor we were stuck with two ideas imposed by our two predecessors. The first was the Doctor's exile to Earth, the second, longer serials – hence 'The Silurians' being seven parts. Both were attempts to save money, both were potentially harmful to the show. Four parts was the best length for *Who*, with the occasional six-parter. And the Doctor isn't really the Doctor unless the TARDIS can go on its travels.

It was the Doctor's exile that worried Mac. After I told him the news he brooded for a moment. You could almost hear the whirring of the computer-like brain. 'Well, Terrance,' he said at last. 'You've now only got two stories, Alien Invasion or Mad Scientist!'

I told him he was being too negative, but as I went home that evening I had the ghastly realisation that he was almost certainly right… And I had a whole season to set up. How could I get away with alternating Invading Aliens and Mad Scientists? I brooded over the problem that evening, that night and most of the following day.

Finally inspiration struck. I called Mac on the phone. 'Suppose the aliens were here all along, a reptile race that evolved before man? They'd regard us as the alien invaders!'

Silence from the end of the phone. I imagined I could hear that whirring again. Then Mac said, 'Yes, I could do something with that.' We discussed the idea further and before very long the storyline for 'The Silurians' arrived. The storyline became a *Doctor Who* serial, and, eventually, this book.

Now about that title. Once the basic premise was established – an intelligent reptilian species evolved before man, went into hibernation to escape a catastrophe that never happened, were accidentally awakened and wanted their planet back – the intelligent reptiles needed a name. Mac looked up a list of prehistoric period names and came up with Silurians.

Later, when the show was in production, Barry Letts had second thoughts. He said the reptiles and apes couldn't have been around together during the Silurian period, and the reptiles should really have been called the Eocenes. Luckily things were too far advanced to change the name, so I gave the Doctor a line to cover the problem.

(Personally I was happy to stick with the Silurians, scientific accuracy be damned. The Silurians sound like a race of malignant intelligent reptiles. Eocenes just sound feeble. Later on, somebody said Eocenes was wrong as well – you just can't win.)

Now, as for the book… and all the other books.

When Richard Henwood was given the job of starting a new line of children's paperbacks, he bought up and republished three old *Doctor Who* hardback novelisations. Reissued in bright new paperback covers they sold amazingly well. Henwood came to the *Who* office and said, 'I need more *Doctor Who* books – who will write them?' 'I will,' I said, and novelised 'Spearhead from Space', rapidly retitled *The Auton Invasion*.

A system evolved that I wrote as many as I had time for – I was still script-editing *Who* – and found writers for the others. The job was always offered first to the writer of the original script - the work was his copyright and could only be novelised by him, or with his permission. If I novelised a script that was not my own – which was usually the case – the money was split fifty-fifty with the scriptwriter. ('I do all the work and you get half the money,' I used to say.)

Strangely enough, not that many scriptwriters were keen to novelise their own script. Scriptwriting and prose writing are very different jobs and many scriptwriters found it hard going. Bob Holmes said it was 'Like digging trenches!'

Mac however was perfectly willing to tackle 'The Silurians' and did, as you'll see, an excellent job adding a few embellishments of his own. I'm very glad that he did and that his book is being republished. Together with the VHS and DVD versions of the show, the book is a fitting memorial to a much-missed old friend to whom I owe a great deal.

The Changing Face of Doctor Who

The Third Doctor

This *Doctor Who* novel features the third incarnation of the Doctor, whose appearance was altered by his own people, the Time Lords, when they exiled him to Earth. This was his punishment for daring to steal a TARDIS, leave his homeworld and interfere in the affairs of other life forms. The Time Lords sentenced the Doctor to exile on twentieth-century Earth. The secrets of the TARDIS were taken from him and his appearance was changed.

While on Earth the Doctor formed an alliance and friendship with Brigadier Lethbridge-Stewart, head of the British branch of UNIT. Working as UNIT's Scientific Adviser, the Doctor helped the organisation to deal with all manner of threats to humanity in return for facilities to try to repair the TARDIS and a sporty, yellow Edwardian-style car he calls Bessie.

UNIT

UNIT in the United Kingdom is under the command of the ever-practical and down-to-earth Brigadier Lethbridge-Stewart. He first met the Second Doctor, and fought with him against the Yeti and the Cybermen. UNIT is a military organisation, with its headquarters in Geneva but with personnel seconded from the armed forces of each host nation. The remit of UNIT is rather vague, but according to the Brigadier, it deals with 'the odd, the unexplained. Anything on Earth, or even beyond…'

From mad scientists to alien invasions, from revived prehistoric civilisations to dinosaurs rampaging through London, UNIT has its work cut out.

Doctor Elizabeth Shaw

Doctor Elizabeth Shaw has an important research programme going ahead at Cambridge when she is invited to join UNIT. Before he encounters the Doctor again, the Brigadier has decided he needs a scientific adviser and Liz Shaw is an expert in meteorites, with degrees in 'medicine, physics, and a dozen other subjects'.

Liz is initially sceptical of the Brigadier's stories about 'little blue men with three heads…' telling him that she deals with facts, not science fiction ideas. But after meeting the Doctor – and experiencing an attempted alien invasion at first hand, she is more willing to accept the unexpected.

1

Prologue: The Little Planet

Okdel stood watching as the last of the young reptile men and women took their turn to go down to safety in the lift. The gleaming metal doors of the lift were set in rock; the doors slid open and shut soundlessly, taking another group of Okdel's people to safety below the ground. Across the valley the sun was already setting, and its last light made the green scales of the young people shine brilliantly. Okdel wondered when he would see the sun again.

'Look, the planet!' K'to the scientist had come up to Okdel and was pointing to the eastern horizon where the sky was already dark. The little rogue planet stood out as a white disc in the sky, lit by the sun. A month ago the planet had been a dot in the night sky. Now Okdel could see it clearly: there were patterns on the surface as though it too, like Earth, had seas and mountains. The little planet was travelling at an enormous speed towards Earth.

Okdel asked, 'Could there be life on it?'

'It's been travelling through Space for millions of years,' said K'to. 'Life is only possible on a planet if it goes round a sun and gets warmth.'

'You are sure it will not collide with Earth?' said Okdel.

'Our astronomers calculate that it will sweep by Earth,' said K'to patiently. 'Our seas will rise up in great waves and for some days the air will be drawn up from the surface of our planet. But the air will come back, and the seas will settle down again.'

Okdel had heard all this before, but he was old enough to know that even scientists could make mistakes. The planet was first seen two years ago. Once the scientists had made the Earth government understand the danger, the government ordered the building of these deep shelters. All over the planet Earth shelters had been built deep under the ground. The scientists could not say how long the population must stay in the shelters – it could be days, or even weeks. So, to save taking down huge amounts of food and water and oxygen, the scientists had invented a system that would put everyone into what they called 'total sleep'. It meant that the people would actually stop breathing. On the ground above each shelter was a device to detect the return of the Earth's atmosphere. Once everything was back to normal, these devices would automatically trigger huge amounts of electricity to wake up the sleeping reptile people.

K'to said, 'Are all the animals safe?' It had been decided to take a male and female of all the more useful reptile animals.

'What?' said Okdel, lost in thought.

'Our animals,' said K'to, 'are they in the shelter?'

'They went down first,' said Okdel, 'I made sure of that.' He paused. 'A pity we are taking none of the little furry animals.'

'You are a strange man,' said K'to. 'The little furry animals are dirty. Insects live in their fur. In any case, this event will rid our planet of the mammal vermin. When the planet draws away our atmosphere, even only for a few minutes, all creatures on the surface will suffocate and die.'

Morka came up beside them. 'Okdel keeps one of the furry animals as a pet,' he said. 'Is that not true, Okdel?'

'It amuses me,' said Okdel.

'Your pet will have to die with the others,' said Morka. 'We shall be better off without them.'

'They raid our crops,' said K'to. 'Our farmers will be glad to see the end of them. But I am sorry about your pets, Okdel.'

'You only say that because Okdel is the leader of this shelter group,' said Morka. 'The little furry animals revolt me! They grunt, they have families, and they are *fond* of each other.'

'It is that quality which makes them interesting,' said Okdel. 'In the zoo I have noticed how they touch each other, and put their limbs round each others' necks.'

'Yes,' said Morka, 'and press their lips to each other's faces! It is disgusting!'

Okdel turned to K'to. 'But as a man of science, do you not find it interesting that a species exists so different from ourselves?'

'Interesting,' said K'to, 'but I do not care to be near them. They also smell.'

'Very true!' said Morka. 'Shall we go into the shelter?'

'I shall follow shortly,' said Okdel.

Morka and K'to walked away towards the lift. Okdel turned and looked again across the valley. The sun was now deep in the western horizon. He wanted to take a last look at the metal domes of the city glinting in the fading sunlight. It was a pity that so many animals were to die. Nearby a huge lizard was quietly munching leaves from a fern. But there was only room in the shelters for a selected few.

Okdel turned to follow the others. Then he heard a familiar sound, and paused to look back into the valley. About twenty of the furry animals were racing across open ground, babies clinging to the backs of some of the females. As always they were calling out to each other, grunting and chattering. Sometimes Okdel imagined they were trying to form words. He was certain that his own pet furry animal understood many of the things said to it, even though it only chattered and grunted in reply. He had released the pet two days ago, so that for what remained of its life it would enjoy freedom to climb trees and race across open spaces.

'Okdel!' Morka was calling from the lift doors. 'We must go into the shelter!'

Okdel slowly walked towards where Morka and K'to were waiting. Just before stepping into the lift, he looked again across the valley to see the tip of the sun as it sank below the horizon. It was the last time he was to see the sun for a hundred million years.

*

Two days later, when all the reptile people were safely hibernating in 'total sleep' in their deep shelters, the little planet swept low across the surface of the Earth. The force of its gravity pulled the seas into huge tidal-like waves that swept over the continents. Volcanoes erupted and earthquakes brought mountain ranges crashing down. Cyclones raged across the boiling seas and the tortured land masses.

But the atmosphere was never completely pulled away from the surface of the Earth. Within a day the greater gravity of Earth had trapped the little wandering planet, turning the course of its flight into an orbit that encircled the Earth.

Millions of the little furry animals were drowned, or swept to death against rocks by the force of the great winds. But some survived. Since there was no time of complete airless vacuum on the Earth, the devices to de-hibernate the reptile people were never triggered.

With the reptile masters of Earth safely hibernating in their deep shelters, the little furry animals – the mammals – were able to live in peace and multiply. As millions of years rolled by, and as the Earth's climate changed and became cooler, the mammals increased both in numbers and in their variety of species. Most of them continued to walk and run using all four

4

limbs. But some, similar to those Okdel saw racing across the valley, began to stand upright on their hind legs, lost most of their body hair, and learnt to use their upper limbs to handle tools. Of all the mammalian species it was this one that learnt how to talk. When this animal looked up into the night sky and saw the little planet still orbiting his Earth, he gave it a special name. He called it the Moon.

The surface of the Earth changed and changed again. Whole continents moved their position. The Earth's crust folded over on itself, not once but many times. The underground shelters of the sleeping reptile people sank deeper and deeper below the surface. In many places rocks and mountains formed over the shelters. The reptile people remained in their state of hibernation, knowing nothing of the world they had lost. They were to remain like that until Man, *homo sapiens*, started to probe beneath the crust of what he now considered was his planet.

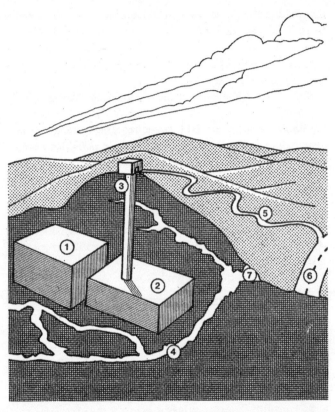

Here you see the hilly countryside, with a part cut away to show what is to be found beneath the surface. (1) the reptile people's shelter (2) the research centre (3) lift shaft going down to the research centre (4) the caves (5) road leading from the main road to the top of the lift shaft (6) the main road (7) the main entrance to the caves.

Horizontal section of Wenley Moor showing cave system and research centre complex

2

The Doctor Gets a Message

Liz Shaw crossed the UNIT headquarters quadrangle as she came from the Communications Office, the scribbled note in her hand. She saw Corporal Grover making for the Armament Room. She called: 'Corporal Grover!'

The Corporal spun round and stood to attention. He didn't salute because Liz was not a UNIT officer, but he stood to attention because she was at least the Doctor's scientific assistant.

'Do you know where the Doctor is?' she asked.

'With Bessie, I think, ma'am.'

'Bessie?'

'You know,' said the Corporal. 'That old banger of his.'

She still wasn't used to a car being called by a girl's name. She thanked the Corporal, and hurried over to the row of garages. Bessie, the Doctor's beloved car, was in the first garage. Liz looked inside. Bessie stood there, her brasswork and shiny radiator gleaming. Liz called, 'Doctor?'

'What is it?' The voice came from under the car.

Liz worked her way round the car, being careful not to step on tools now strewn on the floor. The Doctor's long legs stuck out from under one side of the car. 'There's an urgent message from the Brigadier,' she called.

The Doctor's legs stayed exactly as they were. 'All his messages are urgent,' called the Doctor, 'or at least he thinks they are. Can you hand me the self-adjusting spanner?'

Liz looked in the mess of tools for the spanner, found it, knelt down and poked it under the car. 'Is this it?'

The spanner was taken from her hand. 'Thanks. What's the Brigadier's message?'

Liz said, 'I'll read it to you. It says, "Miss Shaw and the Doctor will report themselves forthwith to Wenley Moor to attend a briefing meeting." That's all.'

The Doctor slid himself out from under the car and looked up at Liz from the garage floor. One side of his nose was black with axle grease. 'Is that all?'

'Yes,' she said. 'It came in five minutes ago.'

The Doctor did not look pleased. 'You can just send a message back to the Brigadier and tell him that I do not report myself anywhere. Particularly not forthwith!' The Doctor slid himself back under the car.

Liz looked down at the long legs and felt like kicking one. Instead she said, 'It's just his way of putting things, Doctor. It's his military training.'

There was no answer from under the car. Liz crouched, trying to peer under the car. 'Doctor? Are you all right?'

'I'm perfectly all right,' the Doctor called. 'This is a very tricky job, under here.'

She straightened up and waited. Then she called, 'Doctor?'

'Yes?'

'It would make a nice trip for us.'

'I dare say,' called the Doctor. 'But I'm far too busy.'

Liz thought for a moment. When she was posted to the job, the Brigadier had warned her never to seem to push the Doctor into doing anything. But this message was *from* the Brigadier: did the warning still apply? She couldn't work that out, so she decided to try another way. She called down to the Doctor again: 'Doctor?'

Silence.

She tried again. 'Doctor?'

His voice bellowed up from under the car. 'Are you still here?'

She said, 'Does Bessie really go?'

For a moment there was no sound. Then the Doctor slid out from under the car, but remained lying there on his back looking up. 'Did I hear correctly?'

Liz said, 'I asked if Bessie really goes. It looks so old.'

The Doctor slowly got to his feet, wiping his hands on an oily rag. 'My dear young lady, Bessie is no ordinary motor-car. Do you understand anything about cars?'

'A bit,' she said, trying not to sound very sure.

The Doctor unclipped a huge leather strap and lifted the bonnet. Beneath, the engine was gleaming, as clean as an engine in a glass case in a museum. 'There you are,' he said, 'twin overhead camshaft, two-hundred brake horse-power, electronic ignition, computerised fuel injection, six cylinders, twin carbs, and polished exhaust ports.'

'That's wonderful,' Liz said. 'But does it actually go?'

The Doctor looked at her. 'Would you care to go for a drive?'

'Really?' she said. 'I mean, yes – I'd love to.' She looked quickly at the Brigadier's message, and added, 'Provided we go to the research centre at Wenley Moor, Derbyshire. I believe the country up there is beautiful, and they've got lots of interesting caves.'

Giving in, the Doctor took the note and read it to himself. 'What sort of a research centre is it?'

'They've got a cyclotron,' Liz said, 'what some people call a proton accelerator. It bombards atoms with subatomic particles.'

There was a touch of sarcasm in the Doctor's voice as he

said, 'Yes, I do know what a cyclotron is.'

'I'm sorry.'

'Is this all the information we have?' the Doctor asked, indicating the note. 'A royal command to report forthwith?'

'That's all the Brigadier said. He just wants us to get there as quickly as possible.'

'I see,' said the Doctor, 'then we'd better not waste any more time standing around here. Hop in.'

'But I've got to pack some clothes,' said Liz. 'And a toothbrush!'

'You might have thought of that,' said the Doctor. 'All right. Let's meet back here in' – he glanced at his watch – 'in ten minutes.'

'But Bessie,' she protested. 'You were doing something to it. Is it safe?'

'Perfectly,' the Doctor said. 'It was just a little gadget I've always wanted… makes a blue light go on on the dashboard if there's ice on the road. Perhaps I could explain it to you…'

Liz cut in quickly: 'Not now, Doctor. I'll get my things – in ten minutes.'

She hurried away to her quarters. If the Doctor wanted to explain his ice-detector, he could do it on the way to the research centre.

*

The Doctor stopped Bessie at the crest of a hill, got out his map and began to study it.

He said, 'You're sure this is Wenley Moor?'

'Positive.' Liz had navigated their journey all the way from UNIT headquarters in London. Now the Doctor seemed to prefer to take over. Liz sat back looking at the great moorland spread out before them. Some miles ahead the land rose into a ridge that continued as far as the eye could see. There were no towns to be seen, only occasional villages and isolated farms.

10

She pointed to the ridge. 'I think it must be over there.'

The Doctor produced a pocket compass, took a reading. 'We have to be sure,' he said.

'I got you all the way through the London traffic,' Liz said, 'up the M1 and off at the right exit.'

'You did very well,' he said, not really listening. He made a calculation on the edge of the map. 'It must be,' he said, making his calculation, 'in a perfectly straight line – there!' He pointed, straight at the ridge of hills.

'That's what I said.'

'Did you?' He put the map away and started the engine again. The six cylinders, twin carbs, and electronic ignition burst into life. They shot forward. 'I rather like map-reading.'

Liz said nothing. They roared along, not speaking, until the road went along at the foot of the rising ridge of land. In a very determined way Liz said: 'It's that track over there.' She pointed to a gravel road that led up the hill from the main road.

The Doctor slowed down, reaching for the map again. 'Well, better be safe than sorry.'

'Over there!' she screamed. 'That rough track. I've studied the route thoroughly.'

The Doctor stopped the car, then turned gently to Liz. 'Do I irritate you?'

'No, Doctor,' Liz said. 'You are the most thoughtful and considerate scientist I have ever worked with!'

He beamed, taking her quite seriously. 'How very kind of you. I hope that our association together will be a long and happy one.'

Liz closed her eyes to stop herself from screaming again. 'Yes, Doctor,' she said quietly, 'let's hope it is.'

The Doctor drove slowly up the winding gravel track. Towards the top of the hill they came to a high electrified fence that went all the way round the hill. A gate was set in the fence with a sign that read: 'RESEARCH CENTRE – GOVERNMENT PROPERTY – KEEP OUT.' Security guards were standing by a little hut next to the gate. One of them came up to the visitors.

'Government property,' the guard called. 'Sorry, you can't come in here.'

'We *are* the government,' said the Doctor.

Liz quickly got out their passes and showed them to the guard. The guard checked them, and handed them back. 'All right,' he said. 'Now give me the password.'

Liz said, 'Silurians.'

The guard was satisfied and nodded to his companions. They opened the gate. One of them called to the Doctor, 'Park that thing over there, then show your passes to the guards by the lift.'

The Doctor turned furiously. 'What do you mean? "Thing"?'

Liz pulled at his arm. 'It was a joke.'

'I should jolly well hope so.' The Doctor put Bessie back into gear, and parked it where the guard had indicated. They crossed to a small concrete building with double sliding doors. Another guard checked their passes, asked for the password again, then pressed a button set in the concrete. The doors slid open, revealing a lift. Liz and the Doctor went inside. The guard grinned at them, shouted 'First stop – Australia' and pressed the button again. The doors closed, and suddenly the lift plummeted down into the earth. Liz gulped, then swallowed as her ears seemed to block up. After what seemed only a few seconds the lift started to slow in its descent, then came to a stop. The Doctor seemed impressed. 'I'd say that was about five hundred feet in three seconds,' he said. Liz just tried to keep her balance, and waited for the doors to open. When they opened a moment later it was to reveal the Brigadier standing waiting for them.

'Terribly glad to see you, Doctor.' The Brigadier shook hands with the Doctor. 'And you, too, Miss Shaw. There's a meeting in progress now. This way.'

The Brigadier strode off down a long metallic-walled corridor. The Doctor took long easy strides behind the Brigadier. Liz had to run to keep up with them.

'How deep is this place?' said the Doctor. 'And how long has it been built?'

Without turning the Brigadier called back: 'Tell you all about it later. Turn right, here.'

The Brigadier did a smart military about-turn at a T-junction of corridors. This brought them to double swing-doors with glass panels. The Brigadier held open one door, put his finger to his lips and said, 'Shhhh!' In a loud whisper he added, 'Take a pew.'

They were in a large conference hall. It seemed as though all the men and women working in the Centre were present. They were all listening to a sharp, clever-looking man who stood on a small platform. He was addressing them rather like a teacher with a class. As they found seats, the Brigadier leaned towards the Doctor. 'That's Dr Lawrence, director of this place.' Liz prepared to listen.

'We are already very considerably behind in our research programme,' Dr Lawrence was saying. 'But I am determined we shall recover our lost ground and go on to make the new and important discoveries that lie ahead. Thank you very much for giving me your attention.' He stopped addressing his audience, and turned quizzically towards the Brigadier. 'Perhaps you could introduce your colleagues, Brigadier.'

The Brigadier rose. 'Certainly, Dr Lawrence. This is Miss Elizabeth Shaw, and this is the Doctor, UNIT's scientific adviser.'

The scientists turned to look at the newcomers. The Brigadier continued, speaking now to the Doctor and Liz. 'This gentleman is Dr Quinn, Dr Lawrence's deputy in this establishment.'

The Doctor turned and shook hands with the small, lean-faced Dr Quinn. 'Very pleased to meet you,' he said. Quinn smiled, and returned the compliment.

The Brigadier continued. 'This, Doctor, is Major Barker.' He indicated a big-built man with a square, ruddy face and close-cropped ginger hair.

'Another scientist?' asked the Doctor.

'Station security officer,' said Barker. 'Regular Army, retired.'

The Doctor shook Barker's hand. 'They must be retiring people very young in the army these days,' the Doctor said, smiling.

Barker looked embarrassed, and gave a quick glance to Dr Lawrence, as though expecting Lawrence to explain why Barker had been retired from the army. But Dr Lawrence just smiled, and changed the subject. 'You no doubt know the purpose of our work here,' he said to the Doctor.

The Doctor said it had been explained to him, adding: 'You send a proton round and round in a tube, then try to hit it with sub-atomic particles.'

'That's good,' laughed Dr Quinn. 'You make it sound like a sideshow at a funfair!' Dr Quinn spoke with the trace of a Scottish accent, and seemed the only scientist present with any sense of humour.

Dr Lawrence said: 'We are on the verge of discovering a way to make cheap atomic energy for almost every kind of use. We are developing a new kind of nuclear reactor, one that will convert nuclear energy directly to electrical power.'

'That'll show 'em!' said the Brigadier.

Everyone looked at the Brigadier, as though he had said something very silly. 'Show whom?' asked the Doctor.

The Brigadier had to think for a moment. 'You know,' he said, 'foreign competitors. A discovery like this will make Britain great again.'

No one seemed very impressed with this, although it made sense to Liz. The Doctor turned back to Dr Lawrence. 'What's going wrong?'

Dr Lawrence explained that a lot of the people working for him had been taken ill, or had had accidents. But the biggest problem was the sudden loss of electrical power to make the cyclotron work.

'Have you any idea what causes these losses of electrical power?' asked the Doctor.

Major Barker spoke before either of the others had a chance to answer. 'It's sabotage,' he blurted out. 'A planned, deliberate programme of sabotage!'

It was obvious that Dr Lawrence had heard all this before from Major Barker. 'Really, Barker,' said Dr Lawrence, his voice strained, 'we have already discussed that possibility. It seems most unlikely.'

'Then why has UNIT been called in?' said Barker.

Dr Lawrence deliberately ignored the question, and turned to the Doctor. 'Look, since you and Miss Shaw have been sent to help us, how about seeing around the place?'

'Delighted,' said the Doctor.

'Good.' Dr Lawrence turned to Dr Quinn. 'You could give them a conducted tour. Now, if you'll excuse me, I must get back to my work.' Dr Lawrence hurried away.

'Ready for the tour?' asked Dr Quinn.

The Doctor said he was, but first he asked what type of accidents people had had at the Centre. Again Major Barker blurted the answer. 'Stupid mishaps,' he said, his face reddening.

'Most accidents are the fault of the people who have them, and there is no exception here. But that's if they *are* real accidents,' he added in a sinister way.

'Accidents or sabotage,' said the Doctor, 'no one has answered my question. What *type* of accidents have people had here?'

'There was a poor fellow three weeks ago,' said Dr Quinn, 'who nearly got electrocuted when the power came on again after a failure. And then three days ago there were the pot-holers.'

'Pot-holers?' queried the Doctor.

'The caves,' said the Brigadier. 'They attract pot-holers. Some of the people here do it in their spare time. Three days ago two of them had an accident – a bit of a mystery, really. A technician called Davis was killed, and his friend, Spencer, is still in the sick-bay here.'

Dr Quinn smiled. 'It's difficult to see any connection between a pot-holing accident and our power losses in the Centre.'

'I agree,' said the Doctor. 'But we should look into everything.' He turned to Liz. 'While Dr Quinn shows me the cyclotron, would you mind visiting this man Spencer in the sick-bay? I may be along later.' He turned back to Dr Quinn. 'And now if you could show me the centre of operations…'

Dr Quinn took the Doctor out into the corridor. 'Where do I find the sick-bay?' Liz asked.

'I'll take you there,' said Major Barker. 'This way.'

Barker marched out. Liz turned to see what the Brigadier was going to do, but he had already settled himself at a desk and was using the telephone. She hurried after Major Barker. Barker marched like a soldier down one corridor after another, all windowless, all with the gentle hum of air-conditioning – air that was being sucked in from five hundred feet above. He stopped at double-doors on which were the words 'SICK-BAY'. 'I'll introduce you to Dr Meredith,' said Barker, and held open a door. Liz entered a well-lit room with a desk, an inspection trolley of the sort you find in a hospital, and two doors leading off to other parts of the sick-bay. Seated at the desk was a good-looking young man writing a report. He looked up, a little annoyed, as Liz and Major Barker entered.

'I wish you'd knock…' Dr Meredith stopped short when he saw it was Liz, a stranger to him. Major Barker followed close on Liz's heels. 'Security check,' said Barker. 'No need to knock. This is Miss Shaw, from UNIT. Wants to see the loonie.'

'My patient,' said Dr Meredith, 'is under some kind of stress. He is not a lunatic.'

'Swinging the lead, if you ask me,' said Barker. 'They all are.'

'*All?*' said Liz.

Dr Meredith explained calmly. 'We've had an outbreak of mild neuroses, psychosomatic ailments, and nervous breakdowns.'

'People pretending to be potty,' said Barker, cutting in.

Dr Meredith ignored him. 'I'm afraid that I won't allow you or anyone to see our latest patient.'

'Then I must insist!' The voice of Doctor Who boomed behind Liz. He smiled to Liz, spoke quickly and quietly to her. 'Just seen over their cyclotron. Very interesting clue there.' But before Liz could ask what the Doctor had discovered, the Doctor was addressing Dr Meredith again. 'Miss Shaw and I have authority from UNIT to see what and whom we wish. I'm sorry to be so difficult, but you cannot refuse to let us see your patient.'

Dr Meredith got up. 'All right,' he said, 'but you do so at your own risk. Follow me, please.'

Dr Meredith opened a door leading to a small passage. Liz went first, then the Doctor. Major Barker was about to follow, but Dr Meredith checked him. 'Just these two, if you don't mind.' He closed the door in Barker's face, turned to the

17

Doctor and Liz. 'This way.'

The young doctor led them down the passage. As they followed, the Doctor whispered quickly to Liz: 'There's a log book in the cyclotron room – they keep in it records of these mysterious power losses. But a vital page is missing, and I could see where it was torn out. The person who kept the log was Spencer, the chap we're going to visit.'

Dr Meredith stopped at the door to a private ward. 'I take it you know what happened to this patient?'

Liz said: 'His friend had an accident in the caves and was killed.'

'It's rather more peculiar than that,' said Dr Meredith. 'Still, you'd better see for yourself.'

Meredith opened the door and they went into a small, windowless private ward with one bed, a washbasin, and as always the faint hum of the air-conditioning. The bed was ruffled but empty.

'Where's the patient?' Liz asked.

Meredith had already crossed to the other side of the bed. 'Down here,' he said.

The Doctor and Liz went round the bed to see where Meredith was pointing. The young man, Spencer, was squatting on the floor, crouching against the wall. Using a felt-tipped pen, he was drawing on the wall, putting the final touches to a picture of a sabre-toothed tiger. There were many other pictures drawn on the wall – buffaloes of a type extinct many thousands of years ago, mammoth elephants covered in fur, and strange birds with scales instead of feathers. In among the drawings of pre-historic animals were pictures of men-like figures, except different from men they had no visible ears and there was a third eye in the forehead. The Doctor knelt down and examined the drawings with interest, while Spencer now sat back on his haunches and grinned like a very small child pleased with his

18

own drawings. Then the Doctor straightened up.

'How long has he been like this?' he asked.

'Ever since he was brought in here,' said Meredith. 'At first he was violent, and tried to throttle me. Then I realised all he wanted was something to draw on the walls with. So I gave him that pen. He's been as good as gold since then.'

'Doctor,' said Liz, 'aren't those drawings like the ones at Lascaux?' Liz had once visited the famous caves at Lascaux in southwest France. Those French caves had been discovered by four schoolboys back in 1942. They were playing a hide-and-seek game, and one of them fell into a deep hole in the ground. He called to the others that he was in some sort of cave, so they scrambled down to see. To their amazement, they found themselves surrounded by drawings on the cave's walls – drawings of animals and hunters made by some Stone Age artist tens of thousands of years ago. The French government opened up the caves so that scientists, and later tourists, could see the remarkable wall drawings.

The Doctor nodded in agreement, then turned to Spencer and pointed at one of the strange human-like figures in amongst the animals. 'What's this one, old chap?' he said in a kindly voice.

Spencer looked where the Doctor was pointing. Then with wild eyes and a groan like a stricken animal, he leapt up from the floor and tried to grab the Doctor's throat. As the Doctor grappled with Spencer, Dr Meredith jumped back in alarm. 'I'll get the guards,' he shouted, and made to open the door. But already the Doctor had Spencer's wrists held in a firm grip.

'It's all right, old man,' said the Doctor. 'Calm down. No one is going to hurt you.'

Just as suddenly as he attacked the Doctor, Spencer slumped back on the floor, cringing in a corner. Dr Meredith tried to apologise for his patient. 'I'm terribly sorry about that. I thought

we had quietened him down over the last couple of days.'

As they left the private ward, the Doctor turned to Dr Meredith and said, 'Tell me about the other man, Davis, who was killed in the caves. Did you see his body afterwards?'

'Naturally,' said Dr Meredith. 'They were late getting back from their pot-holing, so we sent in a search party in case they were in trouble. When they found Davis's body, they sent for me immediately.'

'What had killed him?' asked the Doctor. 'A fall of rock?'

Dr Meredith rubbed his chin. 'I suppose it might have been partly the cause. There was a livid gash down one side of the man's face, and that could only have been caused by a lump of rock falling from the roof. Even so, there was something odd about the wound.' Dr Meredith stopped, as though he felt that what he had to say was too silly.

'What sort of wound was it?' said the Doctor.

'Like a claw mark,' said Meredith. 'You know what it's like if a cat scratches you. But this was a much bigger claw – a claw the size of a man's hand.'

Liz said, 'A piece of rock could have jagged edges, like a claw perhaps?'

The Doctor gave Liz a look to tell her to be quiet, and continued questioning Dr Meredith. 'What did you put on the death certificate as "cause of death"?'

'Under the circumstances,' said Dr Meredith, 'I refused to issue one. There will have to be an inquest to decide on that. But if you want my opinion, the gash on the face couldn't possibly have caused death.'

'Then what,' asked the Doctor patiently, 'did?'

Again Dr Meredith looked embarrassed by the answer he was about to give. He said, 'If you really want to know what I think, the man simply died of fright.'

3

The Traitor

Miss Dawson was worried. She had been one of the first scientists selected by Dr Lawrence to work at the research centre, and she was thrilled to get the job. All her life she had had to live in London, which she had come to detest, because of her elderly mother. Her brothers, older than her and all scientists, had got married and gone to live in America and Australia. Miss Dawson had been the one left at home to look after their ailing mother. True, she had had some interesting research jobs in London, but whenever she saw an advertisement for an electronic scientist needed abroad, or even in another part of Britain, her mother's health had mysteriously taken a turn for the worse. The years rolled by, and people stopped calling her a 'young woman' and said instead 'such a faithful daughter'. Sometimes she met men who seemed to want to marry her; but her mother always knew somehow, and promptly became ill again so that Miss Dawson even had to stay away from work to look after the old lady. In her heart Miss Dawson feared the moment when people would stop asking, 'Why don't you get married?' and replace it with the dread, 'Why *didn't* you get married?'

Miss Dawson's mother had died, of incredibly old age, a year ago. At last free, Miss Dawson immediately applied for, and got, this job at the research centre at Wenley Moor. Derbyshire wasn't exactly Australia or America, but at least it was some distance from London, and it was the start of her new life.

At first her mind was filled with the excitement of the project. To turn nuclear energy *directly* into electrical power, without using a turbine in between, could bring enormous benefits to Mankind. Really cheap electrical power would mean more factories, more hospitals, more everything in all the underdeveloped parts of the world. The research centre was the best equipped scientific establishment she had ever worked in. Her specific task was to release the atoms that raced round the cyclotron tube – a tube so large that the cyclotron room in which she worked was surrounded by the tube.

Dr Quinn joined the team a couple of months after Miss Dawson's arrival. She was immediately attracted to him. He was rather older than her, and had had a terrific amount of scientific experience. Also he was a very kind man, always friendly, and with that trace of a Scottish accent that fascinated her. Above all, he was single. He had been married, but his wife had died in a car accident some years ago. Instead of living in the staff's quarters in the Centre itself, Dr Quinn had taken a small cottage on the outskirts of a nearby village. Miss Dawson quickly made it clear to Dr Quinn that she would be glad to help decorate his cottage and make curtains and even clean and cook if he so desired. With that nice smile of his, Dr Quinn had declined all these offers, but said that he'd be very glad for Miss Dawson to call at any time as a guest.

So the pattern became set. On Sunday mornings, Miss Dawson and Dr Quinn would go walking together over the moors, returning to his little cottage to play at cooking Sunday lunch together. It was after Sunday lunch one day that Dr Quinn told Miss Dawson that he had been down into the caves under the hills, and what he had found there. He had met, and talked to, a reptile man.

At first Miss Dawson refused to believe it. The Age of the

Reptiles ended millions and millions of years ago. In any case, the reptiles never produced a species with a brain larger than that of a present-day kitten.

'I assure you it's true,' said Dr Quinn, filling his pipe and settling back in an armchair, as though he was talking about nothing more extraordinary than meeting another pot-holer in the caves. 'He was well over six feet tall, with green scales instead of skin, and he had a third eye in the middle of his forehead.'

With a lifetime of scientific training, Miss Dawson was not one to accept the fantasy of a talking reptile. 'We know from the fossils that have been found that no such animal ever existed,' she said. 'You must have imagined it.'

'But I've been having conversations with them,' said Dr Quinn, now lighting his pipe and blowing out a huge amount of blue smoke.

Miss Dawson persisted. 'The structure of the typical reptile mouth doesn't lend itself to speech. The most vocal reptile can only produce a very limited sound range.'

'I'm not going to say the fellow talked with an Oxford accent,' smiled Dr Quinn. 'More of a dreary monotone. What struck me particularly was how he could detect *my* language – English – and speak to me in it.'

Miss Dawson decided that possibly Dr Quinn had gone mad. Perhaps he had spent too much time alone since his wife had died. She tried to change the subject. But Dr Quinn just smiled, puffed at his pipe, and went on talking about his reptile men.

'Of course you can't believe it, Miss Dawson,' he said – she had never got him to call her Phyllis – 'because we are educated to believe that the reptiles are a low class of animal with primitive brains. All the fossils tell us that. But what if something else happened, in prehistory, that we know nothing about? For some reason those reptile people are down in the caves, and they've been there for millions of years.'

Miss Dawson asked, 'Then why haven't the pot-holers found them? There are always people trooping down into the caves.'

'Because,' said Dr Quinn, 'the reptile people live in some special shelter they've got there. The one I met showed me the entrance, after I'd promised to be their friend.'

'Their friend?' said Miss Dawson. It was at this moment that Miss Dawson really started to worry.

'They want information,' said Dr Quinn, 'about how we humans live, and where, and how many there are of us.'

'Are you going to give them that information?'

Dr Quinn slowly shook his head. 'I shall play them along, that's all. You see, what interests me is the information that *I* can get from *them*.'

'But surely,' said Miss Dawson, at last believing Dr Quinn might not be mad, 'if you've found these creatures you must let everyone know! It's the most remarkable discovery since...' She was not a zoologist so she didn't know quite who had discovered what living species. 'Well, you know, that fish they found off the coast of South Africa.'

'The coelacanth,' said Dr Quinn, as though giving a lecture, 'caught off Natal in 1938, and thought to have been extinct for seventy million years.' His memory for facts always amazed her.

'Yes,' she said, 'that fish.'

'Tell me,' he said, 'do you know who discovered the coelacanth?'

Miss Dawson shook her head. 'I thought you'd know, since you know all the other details about it.'

'But you know who discovered steam, and gravity, and electricity and evolution?' he said, more as a statement than a question.

'Of course,' she said. 'I don't understand what you're getting at.'

Dr Quinn sat back in his chair and gazed at the ceiling. 'I've given all my life to science, Miss Dawson. But somehow I've always been someone else's assistant, just as I am now assistant to our dear Dr Lawrence, director of the research centre. If I reveal these creatures the world's top zoologists and anthropologists, and probably the Prime Minister and the Leader of the Opposition, will be fighting to get into those caves to be seen on world-wide television talking to a reptile man. In years to come the name Matthew Quinn will be as unknown as – as that of D. E. Hughes.'

'I'm sorry to be so ignorant,' said Miss Dawson, 'but who *was* D. E. Hughes?'

'Exactly!' exclaimed Dr Quinn, then returned to his lecture-hall voice to reel off more information from his mental store of knowledge: 'Professor D. E. Hughes, a professor of music, invented radio in 1879, and built a primitive transmitter in his home in Great Portland Street, London. I bet you thought Marconi invented radio!'

Miss Dawson didn't answer that. 'What do you hope to find out from these creatures?'

Dr Quinn blew smoke and thought for a moment. 'How the world was millions and millions of years ago,' he said thoughtfully, 'what the temperature was like, the flora and fauna. Above all, I believe that they knew the true ancestors of Mankind.'

'What will you do with this information?' she asked.

'I shall publish a paper – perhaps a book. It will be the most widely read book in the world.' He turned and looked at her with his disarming smile. 'Wouldn't you like to know someone who is as famous as Charles Darwin?'

Miss Dawson could see now that Dr Quinn was not the

quiet little man she had imagined. She asked, 'Do you think you can get all this information from your reptile people, and walk away with notes for your book? What do you think *they* are going to do?'

'Go back into their hole in the ground,' said Dr Quinn, 'if they're sensible.'

*

It was some time after this conversation that the power losses started at the research centre. Just as the nuclear reactor was building up to maximum power, all its current would be mysteriously drawn off, sometimes plunging the research centre into temporary darkness. After it had happened twice in one week, Miss Dawson went one day to Dr Quinn's office. She found him looking at a model globe of the world, which he quickly put out of sight in a cupboard.

'My dear Miss Dawson,' he said, 'do sit down. Not that the chairs in this office are very comfortable…'

He produced a metal-backed chair for her, and she sat. 'It's about these power losses,' she said. 'Do you know what causes them?'

'I thought our dear director, Dr Lawrence, was looking after that,' said Dr Quinn.

She nerved herself to say what was on her mind: 'It's got something to do with those creatures you told me about, hasn't it?'

Dr Quinn got out his pipe, then thought better of it and put the pipe back into his pocket. 'The truth is that the enormous volume of electrical power we create down here triggered off the reptile people in the first place.'

'Triggered off?' She didn't understand.

'They were hibernating,' said Dr Quinn. 'I've no idea how or why – they haven't explained that to me yet. But our electricity woke up one of them, and he set about waking up the others.

27

When it suits them, they draw off our power to de-hibernate more of their kind.'

'How have they managed to build cables,' she asked, 'from their shelter to our research centre?'

'They haven't,' he said. 'In some ways their civilisation was more advanced than ours. By induction[1] they can transfer electrical power through earth, rock, anything.'

'You must tell them to stop!' She realised she had spoken like a schoolmistress talking about naughty children.

'I think that's more than my life is worth,' said Dr Quinn. 'In any case, they're not holding up our work too much. And what we're doing here isn't half as important as what *I'm* doing getting to know these creatures.'

'But Dr Lawrence is going to bring in UNIT,' she said. 'Were you aware of that?'

For the first time Dr Quinn frowned. 'No, he didn't tell me. He should have done.' Then he smiled his usual cheery smile. 'Still, we shall have to see how it all works out, won't we?'

'You must tell them to stop,' she repeated.

He looked at her squarely, appeal in his eyes. 'I can't, Miss Dawson. They wouldn't understand. Remember, they think of Earth as *their* planet.'

'But they hid themselves away for some reason,' protested Miss Dawson. 'The Earth belongs to Mankind!'

'They don't think Mankind is very important,' said Dr Quinn quietly.

'But that's ridiculous!'

For a moment Dr Quinn said nothing, studying the neat arrangement of pens and writing pad on his desk top. Then he looked up again, giving that winning little smile of his. 'Miss Dawson, if for some reason you went to sleep in your house for

---

[1] The transfer of electric or magnetic force through proximity but without direct contact.

twenty years, and when you woke up you found the house was inhabited by thousands of mice and rats, what would you do?'

'It's obvious,' she said. 'Get poison, traps – kill them, drive them away.'

'Exactly,' said Dr Quinn. 'And that, I imagine, is what they intend to do to us.'

'Then keeping this to yourself is' – she couldn't think of a strong enough word – 'is criminal!'

'Oh, no, I don't think so. Because, you see, I shall kill them first, after I have found out all that I want to know.'

*

In the weeks that followed that conversation the power losses became more and more frequent. Every time the lights flickered and the electrical output meters registered zero for a few minutes, Miss Dawson presumed that yet another creature in the caves had been de-hibernated.

Brigadier Lethbridge-Stewart appeared with some UNIT soldiers to see if someone was sabotaging the research centre. Both the Brigadier and their own security officer, that red-faced Major Barker, spent many hours together in private conference. Every type of rumour went round the research centre, even the idea that the director, Dr Lawrence, had gone insane and was doing it all himself. Throughout it all, Miss Dawson kept Dr Quinn's extraordinary secret. Although they still met every Sunday to walk across the moors and then make lunch together, she did not even mention what he had told her. At least, not until one of their technicians, Davis, was killed while pot-holing in the caves. As soon as Miss Dawson heard of the accident she went to Dr Quinn's office again.

'I *must* speak to you, Dr Quinn!'

Dr Quinn was making some complicated calculations, and gestured her to sit on the metal-back chair and wait a moment. When he had finished, he looked up to her. 'More power losses,

Miss Dawson?'

'No. Someone's been killed in the caves by one of your reptiles!'

'Not one of *my* reptiles, Miss Dawson,' he said, apparently not perturbed. 'In any case, are we sure?'

'One of our own people is dead!' She was almost in tears. Davis had been a particularly popular technician in the Centre. It was still impossible to think she would never see him alive again.

'Dr Lawrence has already told me about it,' said Dr Quinn. 'Neither Spencer nor Davis were experienced pot-holers. Some of those caves are very dangerous. Perhaps he fell.'

'Then why is Spencer blabbering like a demented idiot?'

Dr Quinn shrugged. 'It's to be expected. If two of you are together and one gets killed in an accident – it's bound to have its effect.'

Miss Dawson was nearly at breaking point. At last she said what had been on her mind for a week or more now. 'You don't mind *what* happens, do you? All you want is to publish that book of yours and be famous!' She got up from the chair. 'I'm going to tell everything I know to the Brigadier, to Major Barker, and to Dr Lawrence!'

Dr Quinn seemed quite unruffled. He simply said: 'If you do, I shall tell them what I know about you.'

Miss Dawson stopped dead in her tracks. 'What do you mean?'

'It's very simple,' he said, as calm as ever. 'I shall say that you found the creatures first, that you swore me to secrecy, but that I finally decided to denounce you because of Davis's death. You, however, said that if I denounced you, you would try to denounce me. Then they'll have to make up their minds which of us is telling the truth.'

'I don't tell lies!'

'I know that, Miss Dawson,' he said. 'But do they?' He paused, then gave that smile of his. 'Look, we've been friends ever since we started working together. Our Sunday mornings wouldn't be the same without those walks on the moors, and cooking lunch together at my cottage. Now why don't we forget all about it?' He made a little gesture to invite her to sit down again, but she remained standing exactly where she was, confused and not knowing what to do. Dr Quinn realised this, so continued with another argument. 'Poor Davis is dead, Miss Dawson. We cannot bring him back. But together we can make one of the greatest scientific discoveries of all time. Incidentally, may I call you Phyllis?'

Miss Dawson sat down on the chair. She had always wanted Dr Quinn to call her by her first name. 'You're a very clever man, Dr Quinn…'

'Oh, please,' he cut in, speaking gently. 'Matthew, if you don't mind.'

'All right,' she said. 'Matthew. But I don't want to steal the fame you are going to have.'

'It's not a question of stealing,' he said, 'but sharing.'

'I have heard something you ought to know,' she told him. 'These UNIT people are going to bring in their special scientific adviser, someone from London.'

Dr Quinn frowned. 'What's his name?'

'I don't know. I heard the Brigadier talking to Dr Lawrence about him. The Brigadier just calls him "the Doctor".'

'Oh well,' said Dr Quinn, 'practically everyone in this place is a doctor of something. One more won't make any difference. At least, I hope not.'

4

Power Loss

When the Brigadier arrived at the research centre he set up his base in the conference room. The research centre was rather like the inside of a warship, in that every square inch of space was used to the fullest. The conference room was the only place where no one worked regularly, so that it was the obvious choice for a temporary UNIT headquarters. He had a telephone installed with a direct line to UNIT in London, and he had his sergeant get maps of Wenley Moor to pin up on the walls. He also had a plan of the entire research centre on the wall behind his desk. He started work by trying to detect some pattern to the power losses – were they daily, or every two days, or weekly? He soon discovered that there was no pattern to them, nor did they relate to any of the work being done by Dr Lawrence and his fellow scientists. The Brigadier then carried out a security check on everybody employed in the Centre, but could find nothing suspicious. So, finally, he called in the Doctor.

Now the Brigadier was seated at his desk, in a plush swivel-chair that he had 'borrowed' from one of the scientists' offices, with the Doctor and Liz Shaw facing him. He hoped sincerely that at least the Doctor could make some sense of the mysterious happenings at the research centre.

'Well, Doctor,' he said, 'what are your conclusions?'

'I was going to ask you the same thing,' said the Doctor.

The Brigadier was never quite sure when the Doctor was joking. He smiled, to show that he thought it *was* a joke. 'Come now, Doctor, I'm not scientist. Just a plain military man. Surely you have some ideas about these power losses?'

'The output of the turbine which is motivated by the nuclear reactor,' said the Doctor, 'is being drawn off.'

The Brigadier studied him. This didn't seem to be getting them any further. 'We know that must be the case,' the Brigadier said, as patiently as he could manage. 'The question is – how?'

Liz asked, 'Have you checked that no one's linked themselves up with the electrical circuits here?'

'My dear Miss Shaw,' the Brigadier beamed, 'my men have checked and double-checked every inch of cable in this entire centre.'

'I thought you would,' said the Doctor. 'Not very imaginative, but correct procedure. I'm more interested to know why that poor fellow Spencer is drawing pictures on the sick-bay wall.'

The Brigadier looked at the Doctor, wondering whether the Doctor had gone out of his mind. So many other people in this place were behaving oddly, although the Brigadier had always believed nothing would affect the Doctor's power to think clearly. 'Pictures on the wall?' he said.

'That's right,' said Liz, brightly. 'Buffaloes, mammoth elephants, and birds with scales instead of feathers.'

'And *men*,' said the Doctor. 'Men without ears and with three eyes.'

'Really, now,' said the Brigadier. 'I saw the medical report on Spencer. It said he'd blown his top after losing his friend in the caves. But this is ridiculous.'

'Perhaps you should have visited him in the sick-bay,' Liz said. 'You'd have seen for yourself.'

The Brigadier tried to put his best face on the situation. He was now convinced that he was talking not to one, but two, mad people. 'Our business at hand, Doctor, and Miss Shaw, is the disastrous loss of electrical power in this research centre. If someone in the sick-bay is drawing pictures on the wall, that is hardly our concern!'

'Do you know,' asked the Doctor, 'what Jung meant by "the collective unconscious"?'

'Jung?' said the Brigadier, 'the psychologist fellow?'

'It's the memory that animals inherit,' said Liz Shaw. 'You know the way a dog walks round and round before lying down, because it thinks it is treading flat the tall grass that dogs lived in millions of years ago.'

'Or the way salmon always return to where they were born in order to breed,' said the Doctor.

The Brigadier was fast losing his patience. 'Doctor, Miss Shaw, this is all very interesting...'

'But you want to know about the power losses?' said the Doctor.

'Thank you,' said the Brigadier. 'Now let's get back to the point.'

'We must first decide,' said the Doctor, 'what the point *is*, and I believe it is connected with our inherited memory of something from long, long ago. There is something close to this research centre which is touching on the depths of Spencer's memory – not his own conscious memory, you understand, but instead the inner parts of his mind which come from man's ancestors of thousands, perhaps millions, of years ago.'

At last the Brigadier had a glimmer of what the Doctor was talking about. 'Something in those caves?' he asked.

The Doctor nodded. 'What is the physical relationship between this research centre and the caves?'

The Brigadier got up, pointed to one of the maps on the wall. 'As you see, the hills rise sharply in this ridge. Inside, the hills are honeycombed with caves, some of them explored, some probably never visited. The research centre is five hundred feet below the top of the hill ridge. For some reason that you probably understand better than I do, the authorities preferred to build the cyclotron very deep in the ground.'

'It's more probably the nuclear reactor they were worried about,' said Liz. 'Just in case it turns into an atomic bomb. Everyone down here would be killed, but it wouldn't do much damage to anyone else.'

The Brigadier hadn't thought of that before. He didn't find it a pleasing thought. 'I'm sure you're right, Miss Shaw,' he said, covering his feelings.

The Doctor was carefully studying the map. 'This means that certain parts of the research centre may be only a few feet away from open cave space?'

'I suppose so,' said the Brigadier.

'Or from anything else,' said the Doctor quietly, 'that might be down here…'

The Brigadier was about to ask the Doctor what he meant when the door of the office flew open and Major Barker entered. 'Brigadier,' he said in his loud voice, 'I must talk to you immediately.'

'Please go ahead,' said the Brigadier, 'although I wouldn't mind if in future you knocked on the door before entering.'

'No time for that,' said Barker. He looked at the Doctor and Miss Shaw, then back to the Brigadier. 'It's private.'

The Brigadier was annoyed with Barker but tried not to show it. 'There's nothing that my two companions can't know,' he said.

'It is *about* your two companions,' said Barker. 'At least, about one of them.' As he spoke he looked at the Doctor, making it quite clear which one he had in mind.

'Have I left my handbrake off in the car park?' asked the Doctor.

'This is no time for jokes,' said Barker, his face turning more red than usual. He turned back to the Brigadier. 'I demand to speak to you privately.'

The Brigadier had had enough of Major Barker. He decided the only way to deal with the man was to be rude in return. 'I demand,' he said, 'that you say what you have to say, and then clear out!'

Major Barker stood there, hardly believing what the Brigadier had just said. For a moment the Brigadier thought the man was going to break into tears. 'All right,' he said at last, 'I shall tell you. This man you call the Doctor is some kind of spy!'

For a moment nobody said anything, not because they were angry but because they were trying to stop themselves from laughing. The Brigadier was the first to be able to speak. 'Have you proof of that?' he asked, in a matter of fact way.

'As soon as your Doctor arrived here,' said Barker, 'I ran a security check on him. He isn't on the files anywhere. Neither the Home Office, the Ministry of Defence, nor even the police have ever heard of him.'

'Because,' said the Brigadier, 'he belongs to UNIT. He's on *my* files.'

Major Barker's moment of glory was over. He had made himself a fool. 'I see,' he said, 'but as security officer of this government establishment, I think I have a right to see this man's credentials.'

'You are absolutely right,' said the Doctor, 'and if I had any I would show them to you. But since we are together again, I wonder if you'd tell me about the "planned, deliberate programme of sabotage" that you mentioned before?'

'It's as plain as a pikestaff there's sabotage going on,' said Barker, taking the Doctor's bait without realising it. 'Anyone can see that.'

'I may agree with you,' the Doctor said. 'But sabotage by *whom*?'

'Communists, of course.' Major Barker gave his answer as though it should have been obvious to everyone.

'Why should communists cause these power losses?' said the Doctor.

'They hate England, that's why.' Barker started to warm to his subject. 'They train people to come here to destroy us.'

'I see,' said the Doctor. 'Are these Chinese communists or Russian communists?'

'There's no difference between them,' said Barker. 'And if it isn't them, it's the fascists. Or the Americans.'

'The Americans?' said Liz, almost but not quite laughing.

Major Barker turned to Liz. 'Miss Shaw, England was once the heart of an empire, the greatest empire the world has ever known. But the bankers and the trade-unionists have destroyed that great heritage. Now we are alone, backs to the wall, just as we were in 1940, only there is no Winston Churchill to lead us. The whole world is snapping at us like a pack of hungry wolves. But the day will come, Miss Shaw, when England will rise again…'

As Barker got more and more excited with his theme, the lights started to flicker. The Brigadier sprang out of his swivel-chair. 'Power loss,' he shouted, and made for the door. 'Follow me!'

The Doctor and Liz sped down passageways following the Brigadier. Major Barker puffed along behind them. By the time they reached the cyclotron room the main lights were already out and the technicians were working by dim emergency lighting from batteries. The Brigadier could only just see Dr Quinn and Miss Dawson working at their control consoles on the far side of the room. He hurried over to Quinn, the Doctor following. 'What's happening?' he asked Quinn. Dr Quinn

37

calmly adjusted some controls, but the Brigadier could detect strain in Quinn's face. 'Power loss, that's all.'

'That's *all!*' said the Brigadier, amazed by Quinn's apparent lack of concern.

Miss Dawson answered for Dr Quinn. 'We're now so used to it, Brigadier.'

'What exactly are you doing?' asked the Doctor.

'Reducing the output of the reactor,' said Quinn, without taking his eyes from the meters in front of him. 'Otherwise the whole place may turn into an atomic bomb, or perhaps you already know that.'

The Brigadier felt someone tugging at his arm. He turned, and saw Liz. 'Brigadier,' she said very quietly, 'come over here. You, too, Doctor.' Without speaking, the Brigadier followed Liz to where a young technician was making notes. He knew the man, a fellow called Roberts, and had already talked to him once or twice. Liz pointed to the notes Roberts was making. 'Look,' she said softly, 'see what he's drawing.'

The Brigadier looked over Roberts's shoulder. Instead of writing, Roberts was drawing a picture of a bison. The Brigadier turned to speak to the Doctor, but the Doctor had already come up beside Roberts. In a friendly voice the Doctor said, 'That's a very nice drawing, old chap.' Roberts looked up, realising that people were watching his picture. He suddenly roared like an animal, and grabbed for Liz's throat. Both Liz and Roberts fell to the ground, Liz kicking and screaming, digging her fingernails into the backs of Roberts's hands as he tried to strangle her. Before the Doctor or the Brigadier could move, Major Barker stepped in, pulled a big service revolver from the holster under his jacket, and brought it down on the back of Roberts's head like a man using a sledge-hammer. Roberts was stunned instantly. With the Brigadier's help, Liz got to her feet while the Doctor inspected the unconscious Roberts.

'You should not have hit him like that,' said the Doctor.

'Only way to stop the blighter,' said Major Barker, now returning his revolver to its concealed holster. 'Anyway, we've got one of them at last. By the time I've finished with him, we shall know everything that's going on.'

The Doctor straightened up. 'I'm afraid you're not going to learn anything from this man, Major Barker. You've killed him.'

5

The Fighting Monster

The Doctor moved cautiously along the cave. He wore a pot-holer's hard helmet, overalls that he had borrowed from a member of the staff at the research centre, and heavy shoes. He was equipped with some strong rope, a map of the explored parts of the caves, a very good torch, and a packet of sandwiches provided by the lady in the research centre canteen. He stopped at a point where the cave passages went off in two different directions.

He called 'Hello?'

It occurred to him that he did not expect a monster to call 'Hello' back; but he wished to draw attention to himself. He stood there listening. The only sound was a distant drip-drip of water falling from the cave roof into a subterranean pool. Of the two passages now open to him, he decided to take the one on the left. That's where the drip-drip was coming from, and, he reckoned, if some form of life existed in these caves it must have water.

After a hundred yards down this passage the Doctor stopped dead. From very close at hand he could hear the heavy breathing of a big animal. The Doctor played his torch along the walls of the cave ahead. Along one wall was a huge opening, perhaps leading to another gallery of the caves. The Doctor crept along to the opening. All at once a huge reptile sprang from the opening, towering above the Doctor. As the Doctor

41

stepped back the torch slipped from his fingers. It remained alight, but fell some six feet from where he was standing. The Doctor moved to get the torch, but the monster reared up over him, its huge lizard-like head swaying from side to side.

The Doctor knew this animal well from times when the TARDIS had taken him back in Time to prehistoric Earth. It was the *tyrannosaurus rex*, the largest flesh-eating animal that had ever existed in Earth's history. Weighing at least seven tons, it stood taller on its thick hind legs than a double-decker bus. Its brain was good for a reptile animal, but pitifully small and stupid compared with the mammals.

The Doctor remained perfectly still. The monster's main interest was the torch, fortunately some distance away from the Doctor. Slowly the great lizard head came down, to inspect the light more closely. The Doctor hoped that if he did not move, the monster, in its stupid way, might not realise that living flesh was but a jaw-snap away. The *tyrannosaurus*'s upper limbs were so short and small to be virtually useless: it could not even reach to put something in its own mouth. So, to investigate the strange torch lying on the rocky floor of the cave, the monster prodded it with its snout. The torch rolled a few feet, and stopped. The Doctor knew that if the monster smashed the torch its attention would soon be diverted to what it could smell – human skin and bone, waiting to be crushed in those great jaws. The monster prodded the torch again, and again it rolled a few feet, this time stopped by a rock.

Then the Doctor heard from far down the cave a strange electronic fluting sound. The monster paused, attracted by the sound. The sound was repeated, following a distinct pattern of notes. Slowly the *tyrannosaurus* reared up to its full height – and then, to the Doctor's amazement, turned round. With an overall length of forty-five feet from nose to tail, this was not easy in the confined gallery of the cave. It first turned its body to face the opposite direction, then curled round its huge murderous tail, so that the Doctor had to jump out of the way. The fluting sound was repeated, and the *tyrannosaurus* ambled off down the cave, obedient as a dog being called home by its master.

Able to breathe freely again, the Doctor reached down to pick up his torch. As he did so, he noticed that in a patch of soft sand the monster had left one perfect footprint. Very excited with his discovery, the Doctor hurried back the way he had come.

6

Into the Caves

At last Major Barker felt that something useful was going to happen. This strange man, the Doctor, had been into the caves alone, and had returned with an extraordinary report about meeting a monster. Well, Barker wasn't fool enough to believe that sort of thing; but at least the report had prompted the Brigadier to organise an armed search of the caves.

'Would you care to come with us?' asked the Brigadier.

It was just what Barker had been waiting for. 'I shall lead the attack,' he replied.

'We're not sure that we're going to attack anything,' said the Doctor. That was typical of the man. If you are going into caves with guns, you are going to attack, or why else go? Still, Barker tried to be agreeable.

'Quite so,' he said to the Doctor. 'But we must be ready for anything.'

The team consisted of the Doctor, the Brigadier, Sergeant Hawkins and a UNIT private, and, of course, Major Barker. All, except the Doctor, carried guns. Barker carried not only his holstered Enfield six-shooter, but also a high-velocity rifle. If there were any foreign spies to be found in the caves, Barker knew how to deal with *them*. As they set off in Jeeps from the research centre car park, Barker felt quite elated. It reminded him of times when he had gone hunting in Africa. To him, those were the good days when Britain still had colonies. It was all over now, of course, but he liked to ponder on those memories.

The Jeeps wound down the rough track to the main road, then cut back across open country to the main mouth of the caves complex. The Brigadier jumped down from the leading Jeep. 'All right,' he called, 'this way.'

Barker was willing to follow at this stage. Later, inside the caves, he intended to get ahead of the others. He wanted to make quite sure that if they found a spy, there would be no nonsense with him. Shoot first, ask questions afterwards. That was Barker's motto.

The little group tramped through the first passageway of the caves, flashing their torches ahead and down every alcove on each side. Then the Brigadier stopped. 'Doctor, you say you found a footprint. Can you lead us to it?'

The Doctor went on ahead. This really tickled Barker. He hadn't liked the Doctor from the start, and looked forward to seeing the Doctor make a fool of himself. After a few minutes they came to a fork, and the Doctor took the left branch. He walked ahead a little way, then stopped.

'It was about here,' said the Doctor.

The Brigadier said, 'No one move, and everyone flash their torches on the floor.'

The Doctor moved carefully towards a small area of flat sand in the cave floor. 'It was here,' he said.

'*Was?*' asked the Brigadier.

'It's been brushed over,' the Doctor said.

Barker could no longer contain himself. 'May I make a point, Brigadier?'

'Well?'

'I'm sure the Doctor thought he saw a monster,' said Barker. 'But perhaps it was some optical trick created by the spies to make an intruder *think* he was seeing a monster.'

The Brigadier turned to the Doctor. 'Is that possible, Doctor?'

'Anything is possible,' said the Doctor. But his attention was now focused on the sand by a rock that came up from the cave floor. 'Those marks in the sand there – that's where my torch was rolled along by the monster.'

The Brigadier inspected the indentations in the sand. 'You could have dropped your torch,' he said.

Barker was glad to note that Sergeant Hawkins and the private were grinning. You can't fool a British soldier, he told himself. No one believed the Doctor's idiotic story.

'I suggest,' said the Doctor, 'that we continue in the direction that the monster ran away…'

The Doctor stopped short as they all heard the sound. It had a strange fluting quality, and seemed to come from a long way deep in the heart of the caves.

The Doctor whispered, 'That's the sound I heard. It's some kind of signal. That's one of the other creatures, calling to the monsters.'

But Barker didn't stay to hear any more of the Doctor's stupid talk about monsters and 'other creatures'. Pulling the bolt of his rifle, he started to run up the cave. The Brigadier called to him, but Barker paid no heed. He could hear that strange sound growing louder as he got closer to it, and he was determined to track down its source. Within a moment he came to another fork, paused for a moment to listen, then hurried on up the passageway where he could hear the sound the loudest. This narrow, winding passage, perhaps once the bed of an ancient river, opened up into a huge cave, bigger than the inside of a cathedral. Barker stopped to catch his breath, and to listen. The sound was repeated, this time from within the cave where he was standing. Then he realised that he could see the far end of the cave, not from the light of his torch but from daylight filtering in from a distant opening to the outside world. Something down there was moving.

'Whoever you are,' he called, 'stop, or I shall shoot to kill!'

The movement, whatever it was, continued. Barker raised his rifle to his shoulder, released the safety catch. He looked sideways at the faint area of light at the end of the cave, a trick he'd learnt from night-fighting. Little by little the unmistakable form of a man appeared at the far end of the cave. Barker held the form in his sights, but decided to give the fellow one final chance.

'If you raise your hands in surrender,' he called, 'I shall take you prisoner, and you will get a just and fair trial in a British Court.'

The man-like form appeared to take no notice, and even seemed about to turn away back into the gloom.

'All right then,' Barker called, 'you've asked for it.'

He squeezed the trigger. The explosion of the cartridge in the confined area of the cave was like a bomb going off. To his pleasure, Barker saw the man-like form reel and stagger. Then, suddenly, something huge reared up from the darkness by Barker. He felt a great claw strike his face. After that, he didn't remember anything.

7

Quinn Visits His Friends

Dr Quinn heard about the armed party in the caves from Miss Dawson. He was in his cottage at the time, having taken home some of his research centre work. The moment he heard her voice on the telephone he knew it was bad news.

'Matthew? This is Phyllis. I need to see you immediately.'

'Where are you speaking from?' he asked.

'The research centre of course,' she said. 'Can you come back here straight away?'

He hadn't thought to warn her that telephone calls in and out of the research centre were probably being tapped by Major Barker. He tried to indicate this now in a way that anyone listening-in would not understand. 'My dear Phyllis,' he said, 'you know how I'd love to be with you at this moment. But the personal things you and I have to say to each other cannot be said in the research centre, with all those other people *listening*. Couldn't we meet in ten minutes' time in Wenley village?'

'There isn't time for that,' she said desperately. 'And if you're thinking of Major Barker tapping this 'phone, he can't. He's in the caves with the Brigadier and some soldiers. They are all armed.'

'I see,' he said. Then he put on his false, woo-ing voice again. 'Well, well, they must be having a jolly time in there. I'll have to get along now, I've got so many things to do. But I'll speak to you again soon. 'Bye.'

He put down the 'phone and thought for a moment. If only those wretched reptile men had kept their fighting animals under proper control, Davis would not have been killed. And if that hadn't happened, no one would have interested themselves in the caves. The worst thing that could happen now was an armed confrontation between the UNIT people and the reptile men. With these thoughts in mind Quinn slipped out of his cottage by the back door, got into his car and drove as fast as he could to one of the cave's minor entrances. On the way he passed the main entrance and saw the two UNIT Jeeps standing there, which confirmed what Miss Dawson had said. Within a couple of minutes he was well out of sight of the main entrance, and was parking his car near a very small entrance in a cliff face which he had found only recently.

He groped his way along a narrow passageway, found a mark on the cave wall that he had put there to remind himself, and proceeded down one after another narrow passage. Finally, he came to the big passageway that led to the main entrance. He was just going to step out into the big passageway when he heard voices and saw the light of torches coming towards him. He held back in the shadows, hoping they would not see him. The little group that went by him was led by the Doctor, who carried two UNIT rifles and the twisted remains of what had been Major Barker's high-velocity rifle, and the Brigadier and two UNIT soldiers carrying the dead or unconscious body of Major Barker. As soon as the group had gone out of earshot, Quinn emerged into the main passageway and headed towards the reptile people's shelter.

At the far end of the large cathedral-like cave, Quinn went up to a huge stone and stood perfectly still.

'I am Dr Quinn,' he said to the stone, 'your friend.'

Nothing happened.

'This is Dr Quinn,' he said, trying to hide the panic in his voice, 'you know me. I am your friend.'

To his relief the stone opened at a crack down its middle, revealing a metal door. As Quinn stepped forward, the hollow stone closed behind him and the metal door slid open. He stepped into a small metal box. In it were two metal stools, and another door that led into the main part of the shelter. Quinn had never been through that other door. He knew he was welcome this far, and this far only. He sat on one of the stools and waited. A few moments later the other door opened and Okdel entered and sat down.

'Why have you come?' Okdel asked. 'It is not the time.'

'I've come to warn you,' said Quinn. 'There have been men searching the caves, soldiers with weapons.'

'Your warning is too late,' said Okdel.

Quinn looked at the reptile face in front of him. It was impossible to tell whether Okdel was angry or forgiving. It was the first time he had really looked closely into Okdel's scaly green face because the sight of it made him want to be sick. 'I was busy,' he said. 'I only heard about it a few minutes ago. You've brought this on yourselves, you know.'

'We?' Okdel sat up very straight, breathing in with an unnerving whining sound.

'If only that human hadn't been killed,' said Quinn, 'and if only you would stop taking power from the cyclotron…'

Okdel cut in sharply, 'We need power!'

'Yes, I know, I know,' said Quinn. 'And I want to help you to have it. But you have already caused too much trouble. There's a full-scale investigation going on.'

'We, too, are conducting an investigation,' Okdel said. 'You promised to supply us with detailed information about weapons and the humans' ability to make war. Where is this information?'

'It's very complicated,' said Quinn, 'an enormous study. There are so many different countries, and thousands of millions of people.'

'Yes,' said Okdel, the green lids of his eyes closing for a moment's contemplation. 'The little furry animals have increased and multiplied.'

Quinn seized Okdel's momentary thoughtfulness to push forward his own claims for information. 'There is a lot of information which you promised to me,' he said. 'Particularly about those little furry animals, my ancestors.'

'You must meet our scientist, K'to,' said Okdel, 'but all in good time. Meantime, this is for you.' Okdel produced a small flat object with various controls, and offered it to Quinn.

'What is it?'

'One of our calling devices,' said Okdel. 'This is how you make it give sounds.' Okdel touched the controls in a pattern, and the flat object produced a fluting sound. 'Your soldiers wounded one of our people, and he had to flee to the surface. You must find him and bring him back to us.'

'That may be impossible!' said Quinn.

'When you have brought him back to us,' said Okdel, 'I may allow you to put your questions to our scientist.' The muscles of Okdel's face twitched three times, which Quinn had come to recognise as a reptile man's way of smiling – except that this time Quinn knew it was a false smile, and that behind it was a threat. 'What is it you really want, Quinn?'

Quinn said, 'Knowledge. To be a respected scientist.'

'We can make you much more important than that,' said Okdel. 'We may not require the return of *all* of our planet. There may be regions where humans will be allowed to continue to exist. To lead them, we need a man whom we can trust. You.' Without a further word, Okdel rose and went away through the inner door.

Quinn looked at the flat object in his hand. Possession of this alone made him the most important man in the world. But what Okdel had just promised sounded even more pleasing. With a little more hope in his heart he rose and went back into the caves.

8

Into an Alien World

Morka had been in the great cave to call back one of their fighting animals when he was shot. By using his third eye, which could see in almost complete darkness, he had clearly observed the strange creature at the far end of the cave. The creature looked to him exactly like the creature that visited old Okdel from time to time. It stood upright like himself, but it only had two eyes and on top of its head was a mop of fur. Its face was pink, almost red. It raised a kind of stick to its shoulder, looked along it, and then shouted something. Then the stick seemed to explode, and Morka felt a terrible pain in his leg. The fighting animal that Morka had come to call into the shelter attacked the creature, and probably killed it – the fighting animals were trained to kill. But Morka wasn't very clear in his mind about that. The pain from his leg affected his brain. All he knew was that he must get out of the cave and that he must once again see the sun from which he, and his people, had been hidden for so long. He saw a patch of daylight somewhere above and pulled himself up rocks to get to it. After that he could not remember any more until he woke up.

He was lying in tall grass. As he opened his eyes he found himself looking directly at the sun, yet it did not blind him which seemed very strange. He remembered the sun as a fierce burning ball in the sky. Now it seemed weak, as though something in the atmosphere was filtering and reducing the power of the sun's rays. He heard a droning sound, and looked towards the source of the sound in another part of the sky. It was an aeroplane. So, these primitive furry animals had discovered how to fly, just as the reptile people once flew in their machines long ago.

Morka slowly got to his feet to get a better view of the alien world around him. Open moorland stretched out on all sides. He had no idea how to find his way back into the cave, and once the weak sun had gone down he would need shelter. It was only with this thought that he realised how incredibly cold he was. Was this the depths of winter, or had the Earth's climate somehow changed? He didn't know. About a mile away he could see some boxes huddled together with smoke coming from a pipe in the top of one of them. Obviously it was a primitive dwelling place, and the smoke came from a fire which the creatures used to keep themselves warm. Morka's ancestors had used fire to keep warm before they discovered electricity. He looked down at his leg. The wound had started to heal now, and trying not to put his weight too much on the injured leg, he started to walk towards the huddles of boxes with the plume of warmth-giving smoke.

He arrived at the farmstead half-an-hour later. Making the journey had been more difficult than he expected. Not only was the sun weaker than he remembered it, but also the air had gone thin. He wondered if, with the geological changes that must have taken place, the reptiles' shelter was now just under a very high plateau, perhaps thousands of feet above sea-level.

A four-legged animal with vicious white teeth came out to meet him. It looked to Morka disgustingly unclean with its long shaggy fur, probably full of little insects. The animal stood growling, baring its teeth. Morka concentrated on it with his third eye. The animal yelped as though hit by a bolt of electricity and slunk away under a farm cart, whimpering. Morka went on

54

into the farmyard. The plume of smoke was coming from the biggest of the boxes, probably where the creatures lived. There was a window and he looked in. Two of the creatures were sitting at a table putting food into their mouths: he was sure one was female and the other male. The fire was in a hole in the wall, and over it hung a stick just like the stick the creature had pointed at Morka in the cave. A stick that exploded and caused pain.

He could have smashed the window and used his third eye to destroy the creatures there and then, but Okdel had insisted that the attack must not start yet. He moved away from the window and crossed the farmyard to a barn. He was already weak again through loss of blood and all he wanted to do was to lie down and rest. In time the others would find him and take him back to the shelter where K'to could repair his injuries. Inside the barn he found long grass which had been cut and gone brown. It made a good bed. He curled up in the traditional sleeping position of his people, and was soon unconscious.

Morka was woken up by a terrible shouting. The male creature was standing in the middle of the barn.

'Doris!' it shouted, 'Doris!'

He seemed too excited or terrified to move from the spot. The female creature came running in. Morka could just see her through the straw where he lay. Through the open door he could see that it was barely light outside and there was a thin white mist.

'What is it?' she said.

'Get on to the police,' said the male creature. 'There's some sort of lizard asleep in my barn.'

'A lizard won't hurt you,' she said.

'It's the size of a man,' said the male. 'In fact, bigger than most men. It must have escaped from some circus.'

Morka's temper was raised. Who did these animals think they were to speak of him like that? He rose up from the straw. The female saw him and screamed. The male spun round to look.

'In God's name,' said the male, 'a monster!'

The male grabbed some farm implement with a pronged end, and immediately lunged at Morka. Morka side-stepped the vicious-looking prongs, grabbed the male creature and broke its neck instantly and painlessly. The woman just stood there, eyes wide, screaming. But she made no attempt to harm Morka, although her screams hurt his hearing.

'Be quiet,' he said. 'You must be quiet in our presence.'

But she continued to scream, and water began to run from her eyes down her pink cheeks. Morka remembered how the ancestors of these creatures always used to make so much noise, especially if you hurt them or if they saw one of their own kind killed. The female creature stood there screaming, hands to face now, its whole body shaking. Morka wondered if it had contracted some disease, and whether out of kindness he should break its neck, too. But his leg hurt and he wanted to sleep. Only then did he notice the hatch open in the floor of the barn. He limped over to inspect it. Steps led down into some darker place below. Perhaps that is why the male creature had come in here – to open that hatch and get something from the area below. Carefully Morka went down the steps, closing the hatch after him to cut out the awful noise of that female creature. Concentrating through his third eye, he looked around himself. It was a small room with wooden racks along one side. He inspected the racks, and found apples. This was good because he liked apples very much. He tasted one, and immediately felt better. Even if the sun was not so hot, and the air was thinner now, apples tasted just the same. He ate a great many apples, then curled up again into the traditional sleeping position and dreamt vividly of his childhood. He had always been good at hunting and as a boy had run with the men hunters when they went into the forests to attack the little furry apes. Some of the boys had kept a few apes in cages, and tried to tame them, but Morka always felt nauseated at their sight and smell. He had killed many thousands of them. Now, perhaps, he would have to kill millions of their wretched, noisy descendants. If they were all like that screaming female creature he had just met, it would be a pleasure!

He was awoken by the sound of feet on the floor of the barn above. The apples had done him good and he had more strength now. There were a lot of creatures above him, probably searching for him with those sticks that explode and make pain. Cautiously he uncoiled and went up the ladder step by step. He put the top of his head against the hatch and pushed gently upwards until there was a thin slit of light. He adjusted his eyes and looked into the barn. Although the faces of the creatures all looked the same to him, helpfully they all wore different clothes. There was a male creature in a long black frock coat, and he was kneeling by the body of the creature whom Morka had killed. Standing close was a female creature with blonde fur on her head – long fur that hung to her shoulders. There were two other males of the species: one in brown clothes, which had fur growing under its nose, and the other in dark-blue clothes with silver buttons.

'His neck's broken,' said the Frock Coat.

The creature with silver buttons tried to stop the Frock Coat from touching the dead creature. 'You really shouldn't touch anything, sir,' it said, 'until the CID has been.'

'This isn't a matter for Criminal Investigation, Constable,' said the Frock Coat. 'This isn't ordinary murder at all.'

'At least,' said the one with fur under its nose, 'the monster cannot be far away. I've got a helicopter up searching these moors. We'll track it down and kill it in no time.'

Another creature dressed in brown came running in. It stopped running and stood very upright, and put its hand to its head. Morka thought it was going to scratch its head, because the little furry apes were always scratching themselves to kill the fleas in their fur. But this action was some kind of signal. The one with the fur under its nose turned and also put its hand to its head.

'Sir,' said the newcomer, 'we've just heard over the radio. The lady found here has come round and is able to talk.'

'Come on, Doctor,' said Fur Under Nose, 'we'd better get to the hospital.'

'One other thing, sir,' said the newcomer, still standing bolt upright. 'They say she's drawing pictures on the wall.'

Fur Under Nose and Frock Coat looked at each other, but Morka could not understand the expressions on their faces. Frock Coat turned to the female creature, indicating a black box on the floor. 'I'll go to the hospital. You'll find everything you need in there for a forensic check.'

Silver Buttons looked very worried. 'Forensics is for the CID,' it said.

Frock Coat turned to Silver Buttons: 'Fingerprints, and ordinary human bloodstains – yes, I would agree. But Miss Shaw and I are looking for reptilian-like monsters.' It turned to Fur Under Nose. 'I'm ready.'

Frock Coat and Fur Under Nose hurried out, along with the creature that had stood upright all the time. Silver Buttons turned to the female creature. 'Anything I can do for you, miss?' it said.

'That's very kind of you,' said the female. 'But I can manage.'

Silver Buttons turned to go, then paused. 'That fellow you call the Doctor,' it said. 'Is he all right in the head?'

'He's very all right in the head,' said the female.

'I'll be wandering around if you need me,' said Silver Buttons, and slowly walked out of the barn.

Morka considered what he must now do. He cursed himself for not killing that screaming female when he had the chance. Now the other creatures would hear from that female how he had gone down into the cellar beneath the barn. They would all come back with their exploding sticks and hurt him again, perhaps even kill him. With those apples in him, he felt that he now had the strength to walk the moors and find his way back into the caves. It would be better if he could wait until dark, but that was now impossible. He looked at the crouched back of the female creature as it opened the black box. It took out some instruments, then went to where he had been lying in the straw. It knelt down, again with its back to him.

Slowly, soundlessly, Morka opened the hatch and climbed up the steps and on to the floor of the barn. The creature was so intent on its work that it did not seem to hear him. Then his foot scraped on the floor. The creature started to turn its head. Morka knew it would start that terrible screaming. He attacked swiftly.

9

The Search

Dr Quinn stopped his car and hurried into his cottage. As soon as he was in the living-room he pulled from his pocket the extraordinary object given to him by Okdel. He touched the controls just as Okdel had shown him, and the device gave off this strange fluting sound. He almost hugged the thing to himself – it was the most important artifact Man had ever known, and it belonged to him, Dr Matthew Quinn. Then he started to hunt through his bookshelves for maps of Wenley Moor. He knew that he had to keep his head and carry out the rescue mission with a methodical search of the countryside. Just in time, he heard the sound of footsteps in the hall and was able to pocket the signalling device. Miss Dawson entered.

'I hope you don't mind,' she said. 'Your front door wasn't locked.'

'Do come in, Phyllis,' he said, relieved it was no one else. 'Would you like some sherry or something?'

'You know I don't drink,' she said. 'I wondered if you were all right?'

'Yes,' he said. 'Fine. Why?'

She looked around noticing the maps. 'Planning a hike over the moors?'

'Possibly,' he said, wishing she would go away. 'Won't you sit down?'

'I was wondering when you'd ask me to,' she said, and sat in her favourite chair. 'Dr Lawrence has been asking where you are.'

Dr Quinn thought for some moments before replying. Then he realised he just had to tell someone his news. 'I've been visiting my friends,' he said, and noticed how Miss Dawson frowned when he said it. 'Look, they gave me this.' He pulled the flat object from his coat pocket, and offered it to Miss Dawson. She only stared at it, and didn't take it.

'What is it?'

'The product of another civilisation,' said Dr Quinn. 'It's a communication device. That fool Major Barker wounded one of them, and they think it ran away from the caves. They want me to help to find it.'

'You won't be the only one looking,' she said very seriously. 'There are soldiers out on the moors now, and they've got a helicopter up. If you go out to find this creature, the soldiers are likely to find you, too.'

Dr Quinn did his best to smile, although inside he was quaking. 'I have every right to go walking on the moors if I want to. We could go together. It would look more innocent.'

Miss Dawson rose. 'I don't think that what you are doing is innocent, Matthew,' she said, 'but let's not discuss that. I just wanted to know that you were all right, and to warn you that Dr Lawrence is on the warpath.'

'To hell with Dr Lawrence!' he said, immediately regretting it.

Miss Dawson touched his arm. 'I know how you must feel, Matthew,' and there was some tenderness in her voice. 'Your father was a world-famous scientist and overshadowed you. Now you are once again playing second fiddle, as assistant to Dr Lawrence.'

'I am not an ambitious man,' he said, knowing it was a lie. 'I only want to push forward the frontiers of science, to do *something* in my life so that people might remember me.'

'I understand,' she said. 'I must get back to the Centre. By the way, there's been some trouble over at Squire's Farm.'

'What kind of trouble?'

'Everybody's being very secretive about it,' she said. 'So perhaps that is where you ought to start looking for your scaly friend.'Bye.' She left.

Dr Quinn quickly looked at his maps and found one of sufficiently large scale to include Squire's Farm. He hurried out of the house, got in his car, and drove as fast as he dared towards the farm. Even from a mile off he could see that something had happened. Parked by the farmstead was an ambulance, two or three police-cars with blue lights flashing, and a couple of UNIT Jeeps. Still, all this gave him a good excuse to stop by. He drove up the farm lane from the road, and parked on the grass verge. Then he wandered in among the public service vehicles. There were police officers and UNIT soldiers standing around, but the situation was still so new and so confused that no one stopped to ask his business. They probably thought he was a senior police detective who had just arrived on the scene. He went up to a soldier and said, 'Where is it?' He had no idea what 'it' referred to, but it seemed the right thing to say. The soldier pointed towards one of the barns at the back and said, 'Over there, sir. In the barn.' Dr Quinn thanked the soldier, and strode across the muddy farmyard to a large barn with open doors. Inside the Doctor was kneeling over an unconscious Liz Shaw, while the Brigadier and some UNIT soldiers were pointing guns down into an open hatch in the barn's floor. After a moment Sergeant Hawkins came up through the hatch with a big torch.

'Nothing down there, sir,' said Sergeant Hawkins, 'except a lot of apple cores.'

Dr Quinn now moved forward, and addressed the Brigadier.

'I was just passing and saw all the vehicles outside. What's going on?'

'There's been one of the cave creatures here,' said the Brigadier, showing little interest in Dr Quinn but instead crossing over to where the Doctor was knelt by the prostrate Liz Shaw. 'How is she?' he asked.

'Coming round,' said the Doctor. 'But she's had a nasty blow across the back of her head.'

'I still don't understand what happened?' said Dr Quinn.

The Doctor turned and looked up at him. 'Some creature killed the farmer, hid in the cellar, and then knocked out Miss Shaw.'

'Good gracious,' said Dr Quinn, doing his best to be surprised. He turned to the Brigadier. 'You've killed it, of course?'

'Unfortunately, no,' said the Brigadier. 'We thought it might be lurking in the cellar, but it's gone.' The Brigadier, again uninterested in Dr Quinn, turned to his soldiers and gave orders. 'I want the whole area searched – outbuildings, the fields, everywhere.'

Sergeant Hawkins sprang to attention. 'Yes, sir!'

Hawkins and the other soldiers hurried out of the barn.

'Anything I can do?' asked Quinn, wishing now to get away but having to pretend to show interest.

'Not really,' said the Brigadier, 'but jolly good of you to offer.'

The Doctor raised a hand for silence. 'Shhhh!'

They all looked down at Liz. Slowly she opened her eyes, looked at the Doctor and smiled. 'Am I still alive?'

'Very much so,' said the Doctor. 'Pulse and heartbeat normal. Can you remember anything?'

'It was a sort of lizard,' she said uncertainly. 'Three eyes. Standing upright. Something wrong with its leg.'

'We'd better get her back to base,' said the Brigadier. 'We've got an ambulance and everything laid on outside.'

'No, it's all right,' said Liz, trying to get up. 'I'll be all right in a Jeep.'

'Hardly comfortable enough for your condition,' said the Brigadier. He turned to Dr Quinn. 'Got your car here?'

'Yes,' said Dr Quinn, trying to think as quickly as possible. 'But I was just going into the town to do some shopping.'

'Really?' said the Brigadier. 'It's half-closing day.'

Dr Quinn again thought as quickly as he could. 'There's one little shop that always stays open. But if you want to use my car...' He trailed off, hoping they wouldn't want to use his car.

'This isn't a matter for discussion,' said the Doctor. 'Miss Shaw *thinks* she feels all right, but she needs rest. Dr Quinn, could you ask the ambulance men to come along here with a stretcher?'

'Really,' said Liz, protesting, 'I don't need *that*!'

But Dr Quinn didn't wait to hear the rest of the argument. He hurried out as fast as he decently could, told the ambulance men to take a stretcher into the main barn, got into his car and drove away.

Five minutes later Dr Quinn was at least four miles away, his car parked on high ground. In the distance he could see the UNIT helicopter. He took from his pocket the calling device and worked its controls so that it played its fluting tune. Almost at once he saw a movement in the long windswept grass a hundred yards away. Then the drone of the helicopter changed. He turned, and saw that the helicopter was flying towards him. Naturally the pilot was curious to know why a man had parked his car in this remote spot. Dr Quinn waved cheerfully to the helicopter, then held up the calling device to one eye as though it were a camera. He pretended to be taking a panoramic view of the moorlands. The helicopter swept low overhead, and continued on its way. Dr Quinn again worked the calling device to produce its fluting sound, and looked towards where he had seen the tall grass move. Morka rose up from the grass, and raised a hand in greeting. Dr Quinn made the same gesture in return, then quickly opened the capacious boot of his car and gave an indication for Morka to get in. Morka slid into the boot and curled up in the traditional sleeping position. Dr Quinn got behind his driving wheel, started the engine, and slowly drove away. At last he had one of the cave creatures at his mercy.

10

Man Trap

Major Barker lay back in his bed in the sick-bay, listening to military music specially piped to him through the bedhead earphones. If he closed his eyes he could see soldiers in brilliant red tunics marching about, saluting their commanding-officer as they went by. He was enjoying just such a daydream when there was a tap on the door and Liz Shaw entered. She had a plaster on her forehead.

'Can I visit?' she asked.

Major Barker immediately removed his earphones, and sat up to attention in his bed. 'Delighted,' he said. 'Do sit down.'

Liz found the only chair available, and sat. 'I'm a patient now,' she said, and told him what had happened. 'How are you getting on?'

'Making fine progress,' he said, although one arm was still in a sling and his head was swathed in bandages. 'You say a lizard hit you?'

'I only caught a glimpse of it,' she said. 'But yes, it was some kind of lizard.'

Major Barker didn't want to disillusion the young lady. There had been talk of these lizards before, and clearly the talk had gone to her head. Young women could be like that – very fanciful. 'I'm sure you *thought* it was a lizard,' he said. 'Care for a grape?' He indicated the huge bowl of grapes by his bed. Liz helped herself to one.

'What do you really remember of the caves?' she asked.

'There must have been two of them,' he said. 'The one I shot, and the one that got me. Has that Brigadier mounted a general flush-out of the caves, yet?'

'Not at the moment,' Liz said. 'The last I saw of the Brigadier he was still at the farm.'

'But in the name of St George,' said Major Barker, 'the obvious thing to do is to go into those caves in force and give them hell!'

'Give whom hell?' she asked.

'The spies.' He paused, and smiled, to make it absolutely clear to Liz that he knew what he was talking about. 'You see, this research centre can really put Britain on the map again. That's why they want to destroy it. It's as plain as a pikestaff.'

'I think you mentioned that before,' she said.

'Because I firmly believe it,' he said. 'Have another grape.'

'They're yours.'

'Then be my guest.' He continued with his argument. 'That was a man I shot in the caves, and make no mistake about it. I called on him to surrender and he ignored me. Anyway, you say there is no armed force down there to defend us?'

'Not at the moment,' she said.

'That seems a jolly strange way to run a war to me,' he said. 'Jolly peculiar.'

The door opened and Dr Meredith entered carrying an official-looking envelope. 'Miss Shaw, I think you ought to be in your own room,' he said. 'And you ought be lying down until you really feel better.'

'But I feel fine,' she answered.

Dr Meredith smiled, but his voice was firm. 'That's an order. Now please, away you go.'

Liz rose. 'Thanks for the grapes,' she said. 'I'll come and see you again.' She went away, and Dr Meredith waited until she was out of earshot. Then he turned to Major Barker with the envelope.

'This just arrived for you, Major. You really shouldn't be upset by anything, so if you'd rather me keep it until you feel better, I will.'

Major Barker reached out with his good hand. 'I'm quite capable of handling my own correspondence,' he said, 'but thank you for being so thoughtful.'

'If you need me for any reason,' said Dr Meredith, 'just ring.' Dr Meredith went away, closing the door.

Major Barker looked at the envelope. On the front it said, '*If undelivered please return to the Chief Constable of the Derbyshire Constabulary.*' He opened the envelope and read the letter. It said:

Dear Sir,

The recent death of Mr George Roberts, employed as a technician at the Research Centre, Wenley Moor, has been brought to our attention by your director, Dr Lawrence, in the normal course of events. We understand that he was struck a blow on the back of the head, when suffering from a fit. We understand that you are unwell at the moment. However, when you are fit we should be pleased if you will get in touch with us in order to assist us with our enquiries.

We are,

Your Obedient servant,

Chief Constable.

Major Barker held the letter first one way then another to try to read the signature. But it was just a set of three squiggles and could have meant anything. Then he put the letter to one side and started to think what it really meant.

68

Of all ridiculous things, he was going to be blamed for killing that idiot technician, Roberts. After all, the man had clearly gone mad and was attacking Miss Shaw. Instead of clubbing the man, he should have shot him outright. Now there was going to be an enquiry, and he would be blamed for hitting the man too hard.

He sat back in his bed and closed his eyes again. This time instead of seeing soldiers in brilliant red tunics he saw himself, one rainy day in Londonderry, Northern Ireland, leading a group of soldiers who were trying to pin down an IRA sniper. The sniper had already shot two of his men dead, and wounded a third. The Major carefully worked his men into a position so that the sniper was completely surrounded. Then he called upon the sniper to surrender. A rifle was thrown down from a window, and a man appeared with his arms raised. As Major Barker called on his men to break cover and arrest the sniper, shots rang out from a sniper in another building, instantly killing the young soldier next to Major Barker. Without a second's thought, Barker aimed his revolver at the sniper standing with his hands up in surrender, and shot him dead. For that moment of anger, Major Barker had been asked to resign from the British Army and to find another job.

Now he could see that it was all going to happen again. For doing his job, for protecting Miss Shaw from the lunatic Roberts, he would be dismissed from the research centre, perhaps even sent to prison this time. Meanwhile, the spies were gathering their numbers in the caves, people out to do harm to England.

All at once he pulled away the bandages from his head, ripped off the sling holding his battered arm, and got out of bed. They hadn't taken his clothes away, thank goodness. He found them in a cupboard, and quickly put them on. In fear they had taken his keys, he felt the right-hand pocket of his

69

jacket. But he was in luck: his precious keys were still there. He quietly slipped out of the room, down the sick-bay corridor into one of the main parts of the research centre. A UNIT soldier passed him, but they both nodded to each other, the soldier not realising that this was Major Barker.

Fortunately, there was no guard on the gun cupboard. Barker undid the lock, opened the cupboard and selected an FN .303 and cartridges to match. Then he went along to the lift. This would be the tricky bit. But again he was in luck. The lift was in the 'down' position, its doors wide open. He walked in, pressed the button marked 'surface', and within a few seconds stepped out into the clean Derbyshire air above. Here there was a guard, one of the UNIT men. The soldier stepped forward.

'Beg your pardon, sir,' the soldier said, 'but where are you taking that rifle?'

Major Barker didn't hesitate. 'I'm chief security officer here,' he said, telling the absolute truth, then following it with a terrible lie. 'Your Brigadier has got trouble on his hands at a nearby farmstead. He radio'd in for me to go and help him, and said I should be armed.'

The soldier looked uncertain. 'Well, sir, he should have let me know. I'm only new here. Have you got an identity card?'

'Of course I have,' said Barker, 'and very correct of you to ask for it. Hold my rifle a moment.' Barker thrust the rifle into the surprised soldier's hands, as though he needed both hands free to find his identity card. He patted his pockets, then gave the soldier a big smile. 'How silly of me. I've got it in the pocket of another jacket.' The soldier smiled back, and offered Barker his rifle. Barker seemed about to take it, then quickly hit the soldier on the chin. The soldier fell first to his knees, then collapsed completely. Barker took back his rifle, hurried over to his car, got into it, and drove at break-neck speed down the twisting rough lane to the main road. Once on the main road he swerved off towards the main opening of the cave. He grabbed a torch from the car's glove pocket, loaded his rifle, and hurried into the cave.

Once inside the cave he started to call his challenge to the enemy. 'If you are real men, come out shooting!' He stopped, and listened. The only sound was the persistent drip-drip of water. Barker plunged on further into the caves, flashing his torch, his rifle always at the ready. He stopped again. 'I know you hate England. But there are some true patriots around, people who love their country. Surrender now and you will all get a just trial!' He listened. Again nothing but the drip-drip of distant water.

'I know you're here!' he shouted. 'I got one of you yesterday! He was foolish, didn't do what I told him. But I'll give you all a chance if you'll reveal yourselves!'

Silence.

Major Barker took another step forward. 'All right, then I

shall kill every one of you...' His words ended in a terrible scream. A metal trellis had sprung up from the soft sand, trapping both his ankles. He looked down almost in tears, afraid that his feet would be cut off. Then he heard them coming to get him. He flashed his torch wildly, and saw lizard-like faces advancing towards him.

'It's no good dressing up in those funny clothes,' he screamed. 'Fancy-dress isn't going to save you.'

Fumbling with the bolt of the rifle, he raised it and took aim at a lizard face. The third eye of the lizard face suddenly glowed a brilliant red, and Major Barker felt his rifle knocked from his hands.

'All right,' he screamed as they finally closed in on him, 'kill me now. I die for England and St George!'

11

The Doctor Makes a Visit

The Doctor and the Brigadier stood looking at the flattened tall grass.

'Something has lain down here,' said the Brigadier. He looked across the moor. 'They don't have cows here, and the pattern is too big for a dog or a sheep.'

The Doctor had already thought of all that. He was more interested in the track of flattened tall grass leading to a rough moor road. As he neared this road he could clearly see footprints, and pointed them out to the Brigadier.

'Anything like that footprint you claim to have seen in the cave?' asked the Brigadier.

'No,' said the Doctor. 'Much smaller. You see, there are two sorts of creatures in those caves.'

The Brigadier gave the Doctor an unbelieving look, but said nothing. They walked along a little further, studying the reptile man's footprints. 'He must have been prepared for a jolly long walk,' said the Brigadier eyeing the road as it went off in a dead straight line across the moor.

'Except that he didn't walk very far,' said the Doctor. 'You see, the footprints end here.'

The Brigadier looked. 'By jove, so they do! Do you think these things can fly?'

'Possibly,' said the Doctor. He had noticed something else strange – the fresh prints of car-tyre treads. 'Could I borrow a

Jeep?' he asked.

'I thought you'd got Bessie,' said the Brigadier.

'She's at the research centre,' said the Doctor. 'You've got two Jeeps standing over there. I only want one of them.'

The Brigadier looked resigned. 'Permission to use Jeep – granted.'

'Thank you,' said the Doctor, and hurried away to the waiting Jeeps.

'Hey,' called the Brigadier. 'What do we do about these footprints?'

'Take plaster-casts,' the Doctor called back. 'Send them to Scotland Yard and see if they belong to any known criminal. See you later.'

The Doctor jumped into one of the Jeeps, turned on the engine and drove at high speed across the open moor. Within a minute the Brigadier and his soldiers were tiny figures receding into the distance. Once well out of sight of them, the Doctor swung round in the direction of Dr Quinn's cottage.

Dr Quinn's car was parked at the back of the cottage. The Doctor parked the Jeep beside it, got out, produced a handkerchief and loudly blew his nose. Then he dropped the handkerchief, as close as he could to one of the wheels of Dr Quinn's motor-car. As the Doctor knelt down to pick up his handkerchief he took a good look at the tread pattern of the car tyres. Then he straightened up, pocketed his handkerchief, and went round to the front door. On the second knock, Dr Quinn opened the door. He tried to look pleased to see the Doctor, but obviously wasn't.

'Hello, Doctor,' he said, 'this is an unexpected pleasure.'

'I just happened to be passing,' said the Doctor. 'What a charming little cottage you have here! Mind if I see inside?'

Dr Quinn automatically stepped back to let the Doctor enter. 'Yes, if old houses interest you – by all means.'

'They do,' said the Doctor, enthusiastically, 'they do. How old is this one – two hundred years?'

By now the Doctor had wandered into the main living-room, Dr Quinn following him. 'The estate agent thought it was older,' said Dr Quinn.

'So you've bought it?' said the Doctor. 'You're not renting it?'

'It was the only way to get a place,' said Dr Quinn. 'It cost rather a lot, but it was worth it. I got tired of living in those quarters they let us have at the research centre.'

'Wise man,' said the Doctor. He was looking about the place with great curiosity. 'You've had quite a bit done, haven't you?'

'A few things,' said Dr Quinn. Then he glanced at his watch and said, 'Look, I'm awfully sorry, but I shall have to get on with some work.'

The Doctor ignored this. 'Did you have the central-heating put in?' he asked.

Dr Quinn nodded. 'Yes. It gets very cold here in winter, so I'm told.'

The Doctor licked his index finger, held it up, and thought for a moment. 'I'd say it's at least thirty-three degrees in this room. Most people would find that uncomfortably hot.'

'The thermostat has jammed,' said Dr Quinn. 'Now I must get on with my work…'

'If you've got trouble with your central-heating thermostat,' said the Doctor, striding back into the hall, 'lead me to it. You can be getting on with your work while I fix your central-heating, I like tinkering with things. Where is it?'

By now Dr Quinn was perspiring and not only through the heat. 'Where is *what*?' he asked a little irritably.

'The thermostat,' said the Doctor. 'The place is as hot as the reptile-house in the zoo. It's very unhealthy.' The Doctor looked around the hall, and saw a door under the stairs. 'Is that where it is?' He made to open the door, tried the handle and found it locked.

'That is just a store-room,' said Dr Quinn. 'The thermostat is in there, but I'd much rather you left it alone. It's still under guarantee, you see. I must call in the people who installed it.'

The Doctor stopped and turned to smile at Dr Quinn. 'Wise fellow. If I tamper with it you will break the conditions of the guarantee.'

'Exactly,' said Dr Quinn, clearly much relieved.

'I shall leave you in peace then,' said the Doctor, going towards the front door. 'By the way, are you related to Sir Charles Quinn?'

'He's my father,' said Dr Quinn.

'He did a great deal of the early work on smashing the atom,' said the Doctor. 'No wonder you went into nuclear physics.'

'There was no option,' said Dr Quinn. 'One didn't argue with my father.'

The Doctor paused on the doorstep. 'Oh? Did you want to do something else?'

'As a boy I was interested in geology. My father thought that rather childish. Learning about the history of our planet doesn't *do* anything, like making wheels go round.'

The Doctor felt rather sorry for Dr Quinn. 'I imagine being the son of a famous scientist isn't easy,' he said.

Dr Quinn tried to cheer himself up with a smile. 'Oh, I don't know. I may be famous myself one day. In science you never know what's going to happen next.'

'That's true,' said the Doctor. 'You never know. Well, thank you for letting me see inside your charming house. I shall have to get along.'

The Doctor went back to the Jeep and drove away slowly. He knew that Dr Quinn was hiding something, but he didn't know why. As soon as he got back to the research centre he found Liz, and told her of his suspicions about Dr Quinn, and started to search the man's office. Liz was nervous. 'What if he comes back and catches us in here?' she said.

'He won't be coming back,' said the Doctor, opening the drawers of Dr Quinn's desk, 'at least not for the time being. I believe he's got a visitor in that little house of his, someone who needs to be kept very warm.' The Doctor took from a drawer the cast of a fossil. 'Look, a *trilobite*.'

Liz looked. 'The first animals that came up from the sea. Why is he interested in fossils?'

'It's his first love,' said the Doctor, turning his attention now to a cupboard. 'He didn't really want to be a physicist...' His voice trailed off as he found a sheaf of papers in the cupboard and started to read them. 'These are notes he's made about the beginning of life on this planet.'

Liz looked into the cupboard, took out a plastic ball with markings on it. 'Surely these marks mean something?' she said.

The Doctor looked at the ball for a moment. 'It's a crude globe of the Earth when all the land masses were joined together. You see,' he said, pointing, 'there is the western outline of the Americas. That's how the Earth was before the Great Continental Drift, two hundred million years ago.'

They both looked at the globe in wonder, and didn't notice Miss Dawson as she entered the office. In a loud voice she asked, 'Have you Dr Quinn's permission to be in here?'

The Doctor and Liz spun round, caught red-handed. The Doctor put on his most charming smile. 'As a matter of fact, no,' he said. 'But I must find out what is going on here before anyone else is killed.'

'If you're talking about the pot-holer,' said Miss Dawson, with rising anger, 'I don't see that gives you any excuse to pry into another person's personal possessions.'

'Not only the pot-holer, Miss Dawson,' said the Doctor, 'but now a local farmer. The question is, who will be next?'

The Doctor paused to see Miss Dawson's reaction. He realised by her look that she was a very worried woman. So he pressed home his attack a little more. 'I believe that you and Dr Quinn are very good friends. Is that correct?'

She nodded.

'Then you ought to know,' he said, 'that Dr Quinn is in grave trouble, and possibly in great danger.'

Miss Dawson thought for a few moments. Then she said, 'I warned him. I tried to tell him.'

'Tell him what?' said the Doctor.

Again Miss Dawson thought before speaking. 'I promised not to tell anyone. You see, Dr Quinn is on the verge of a great discovery, perhaps the most important scientific discovery any man has ever made.'

'I am a man of science,' said the Doctor. 'You must trust me and tell me everything you know.'

'All right,' she said. 'If you really think Dr Quinn is in danger, I'll tell you…'

The Brigadier rushed into the office. 'Where the devil have you been, Doctor? We're due for a meeting with Dr Lawrence in a minute!' Then he stopped dead as he realised he had walked into a conversation between the Doctor and Miss Dawson. 'Oh, sorry. Something going on?'

The Doctor said quietly, 'Miss Dawson, you were going to tell me something.'

Miss Dawson looked from the Doctor to the Brigadier, then back to the Doctor. 'I'm sorry, Doctor. My first loyalty is to my friend. If you'll excuse me.' She hurried out of the office.

The Brigadier looked perplexed. 'What on earth was that all about?'

'Nothing,' said the Doctor. 'Just a cosy chat about the weather. Now, shall we go to this meeting?'

12

Goodbye, Dr Quinn

As Miss Dawson went up in the research centre lift she could feel the blood pounding in her temples. She had almost been disloyal to Dr Quinn. If she had said what she knew, he might be in very serious trouble. Once at the surface, she almost ran to her little car in the car park, then drove as fast as possible down to Dr Quinn's cottage. She pounded on the front door and kept on pounding until she heard Dr Quinn calling from the other side.

'For goodness' sake, who is it?'

'It's me,' she screamed, 'Phyllis. You must let me in!'

She heard the rattle of the door chain and then the mortice-lock being turned. Normally, Dr Quinn never locked his front door, as did anyone in this wild countryside. She almost fell into the hallway.

'My dear girl,' said Dr Quinn. 'What's all the bother?' He held her in his arms in a gentle embrace. She was aware of her own heart-beats and the fact that she was gasping for breath. 'It's as if the Devil himself were on your tail,' he laughed.

Miss Dawson caught her breath and straightened up. Then she noticed the heat. 'Why is it so warm here?' she asked.

'Is that all you've come to say to me?' he said. 'Now come into the living-room and take your coat off.'

They went into the living-room, and Dr Quinn helped her with the jacket of her suit. 'Sit yourself down, lass,' he said soothingly, 'have a nice, quiet sherry and tell me what's on your mind.'

She sat, but only on the edge of a chair. Dr Quinn poured a couple of sherries. 'The Doctor knows what you're doing,' she said.

Dr Quinn didn't seem at all put out. He continued to pour the two glasses of sherry and then brought them over to where Miss Dawson was sitting perched on the chair. 'Really?' he said. 'Is that what he told you?'

'He was searching your office.' Miss Dawson sipped at the sherry but somehow didn't want to drink it. 'He talked to me. He wants to help you.'

'Does he indeed?' said Dr Quinn, seemingly amused. 'He wants to steal the credit for my discoveries.'

'You haven't discovered anything yet,' she said. 'Can't you turn down the central-heating?' She could scarcely breathe.

'I'm feeling a bit of a chill coming on,' he said, 'so I want to keep warm. I'd say that I've discovered rather more than most people. An entirely separate species of intelligent life.'

'But you can't make them tell you anything!'

Dr Quinn looked into the sherry in his glass. 'Can't I? Phyllis, I've got one of them here.'

Alarmed, Miss Dawson looked round. 'Where?'

'Oh, not roaming around the house,' he said with that smile of his. 'It's the one they're hunting. I've got it locked up safe and sound in the store-room.'

'But it's killed somebody,' she said. 'It might kill you!' She realised how terribly fond she was of Dr Quinn, even if she had started to doubt whether he was at all fond of her.

'It's wounded and it's weak,' he said. 'I have the key to the situation,' and he produced a big old-fashioned key and laughed. 'If it wants out, if it even wants food, it's got to tell me what I want to know. It needs heat to stay alive, and it needs to be fed.'

'Do you really believe you can make a deal with a monster?' she asked.

'It's a matter of common sense,' he said. 'The other reptiles don't know where it is, and it doesn't know how to get back to their shelter in the caves. So, unless it's willing to co-operate I'm going to starve it and turn off the central-heating.'

'You might start doing that now,' she said. She sniffed. 'I can smell burning. Are you sure the central-heating is safe?'

'I've had it full on before...' Dr Quinn stopped, and also sniffed. 'Just a moment.' He got up and opened the door to the hall. A cloud of smoke poured in from the hall. Dr Quinn stood there as though he could not believe what he was seeing.

'What is it?' said Miss Dawson.

'It's breaking out,' he said, and seemed unable to move from where he was standing.

Miss Dawson rushed over to the door. The hall was full of smoke. Through the smoke she could see the door to the store cupboard glowing red with heat. Suddenly the door completely disintegrated into a mound of brilliantly red ashes and the reptile man stepped through into the hall. The third eye in its forehead was glowing as brilliantly as the embers at its feet.

'I'm going to help you,' Dr Quinn said. 'I was going to bring you food and water, and take you back to your people...' Dr Quinn's words ended in a strangled scream as the reptile man turned to face him. The third eye glowed a more brilliant red for a few seconds, and Dr Quinn crumpled to the floor and was silent.

'Please,' said Miss Dawson, 'please don't kill me. I mean you no harm. I want to live. Don't kill me, please.'

The glow of the third eye subsided.

'You are intruders on our planet,' said the reptile man. 'You will all die eventually.' He walked slowly across the hall, one

arm raised. Miss Dawson nerved herself for the blow. The palm of the reptile hand hit her across the side of her face, and she fell unconscious on top of Dr Quinn.

13

The Prisoner

The Doctor, the Brigadier, and Liz sat on hard-backed chairs in front of Dr Lawrence's desk. Dr Lawrence was a very angry man. 'I just don't understand what you think you're doing,' he said, directing his remark to the Brigadier. 'You came down here to deal with the problems which I set out in my paper to the Minister. All you've done is chase about in the caves, and mount some sort of man-hunt in the surrounding countryside. On top of all that, you have allowed that fool, Major Barker, to escape from the sick-bay and knock out one of your own guards.'

The Brigadier said, 'I agree that we haven't got very far with our investigation, Dr Lawrence…'

Dr Lawrence cut in without listening to the rest of what the Brigadier might have said. '"Haven't got very far"? That is the understatement of the century! We are still suffering from these power losses. You have come up with no explanation about that!'

The Doctor said, 'I believe the power is being drained off by some means we don't understand yet.'

Dr Lawrence turned and looked at the Doctor. 'My dear sir, even I could have told you that!'

'The problem,' said the Brigadier, 'seems to lie in the caves.'

'If only the research centre had been built somewhere else,' said Liz, not very helpfully. 'You see, that's the trouble.'

Dr Lawrence tried to hold back his anger. 'Miss Shaw, this research centre has cost the government twenty million pounds to construct. Of one thing you may be certain – we are not going to move to another site!'

The Doctor quickly tried to cover for Liz. 'I'm sure my companion didn't mean to suggest that, Dr Lawrence. But the construction of this centre in the same hill as these particular caves does seem rather unfortunate...' The Doctor stopped as Dr Meredith came rushing into the office.

Dr Meredith started to speak. 'Dr Lawrence...' But Dr Lawrence waved him to silence and looked at his wristwatch.

'You are exactly eighteen minutes late,' said Dr Lawrence. 'I called this meeting for three o'clock.'

'I was looking for Major Barker,' said Dr Meredith, clearly flushed with some news he wanted to impart. 'I thought he might have gone to Dr Quinn's cottage, so I just called there.' He paused to catch his breath. 'Dr Quinn's dead, and Miss Dawson is behaving just like Spencer, cringing in a corner of the hallway, unable to talk.' Dr Meredith slumped into the one remaining hard-backed chair. 'There's something else,' he went on. 'The door from Dr Quinn's store-room to the hall has been burnt down.'

For a moment no one said anything. Liz looked to the Doctor, but the Doctor pretended not to notice her look. It was the Brigadier who broke the silence. 'I shall send a request for more troops,' he said calmly, 'many more troops, so that we can enter those caves and find out exactly what's going on.'

'I'd much rather if you didn't do that,' said the Doctor. 'A full-scale military action could be absolutely disastrous.'

'I believe you are UNIT's scientific adviser,' said Dr Lawrence, 'and not a military man. I completely endorse the Brigadier's plan. If, as Major Barker claimed, there are saboteurs in those caves, enemies of this country, they must be routed.'

'Thank you, sir,' said the Brigadier, rising. He turned to the Doctor. 'I'm sorry, Doctor. It's the only way.' Without waiting for a reply, the Brigadier hurried out.

Dr Lawrence also rose. 'The meeting is closed. And now I must get on with trying to run this research centre.' He hurried out after the Brigadier.

The Doctor turned to Dr Meredith. 'Do you know how Dr Quinn was killed?'

Dr Meredith shook his head. 'So far as I could see, there wasn't a mark on his body. His heart had just stopped beating. But I'm going back there to make a full report.'

Liz asked, 'What's happened to Miss Dawson?'

'I called the ambulance,' said Dr Meredith. 'She's been taken to the local cottage hospital.' He paused a moment, as though not entirely believing what he was about to say. 'You remember how Spencer drew pictures on the wall? She was doing the same. She was cringing in a corner, sticking her finger into the black ash of what had been the store-room door, and drawing pictures on the wall. The same pictures of animals and men.' He drew a deep breath, then slowly got to his feet. 'Well, since the meeting's over, I'd better get back to the cottage,' he said and went to the door. 'Tell me, Doctor, have you any idea why these people draw pictures on the wall?'

'I think it's got something to do with race-memory,' said the Doctor. 'There was a time when Man was very weak and always at the mercy of the same terrible enemy, just as mice are always afraid of cats.'

Dr Meredith looked rather uncertain about that idea. 'Well,' he said, 'it's something I've never met with in the medical text-books before. Any idea how I should cope?'

'Tender, loving care,' said the Doctor. 'I believe that's the correct nursing term.'

Dr Meredith smiled. 'Yes, indeed,' he said. 'When in doubt,

TLC.' He left the office.

'Well,' said Liz, 'that seems to settle that.'

'That,' said the Doctor, 'seems to settle what?'

'The Brigadier is going to call in lots more troops,' said Liz. 'He'll invade the caves and find out what's really there. Then we can all go home.'

'You can go where you like,' said the Doctor, 'but I'm going to go into those caves before we have a major war on our hands.'

'What do you hope to do there?'

'Make peaceful contact with whatever is in there,' the Doctor said, and rose to go.

Liz also got up. 'All right. Then we go together.'

'Oh no,' said the Doctor. 'I think this is something I have to do on my own, thank you.'

'Doctor,' said Liz, stopping him in his tracks with the tone of her voice, 'if the Brigadier knew you were going into those caves he'd stop you.'

'No one's going to tell him,' said the Doctor.

'I am,' said Liz, 'unless I'm going with you.'

'You realise this is blackmail,' he said.

'That's right,' she said. 'We started this together, so let's finish it together.'

The Doctor shook his head in despair. 'Since I have no alternative,' he said, and then smiled, 'let's go and find some monsters.'

*

The Doctor and Liz went along the main passageway of the caves leading from the entrance. The Doctor paused, pulled from his pocket papers he had taken from Dr Quinn's office. He opened up a folded paper to reveal a crudely drawn map. Liz shone her torch on it. The Doctor pointed his finger to an X which Dr Quinn had marked on the map. 'That, presumably, is where we've got to make for,' he said.

'All right,' said Liz, 'let's go.' She shone her torch back to the route ahead of them, then noticed something on the cave floor glint in the light of the torch. The Doctor also noticed it, went and picked it up and inspected it.

'A cartridge from an FN .303 rifle,' said the Doctor. He held it close to his nose and sniffed. 'Recently fired.'

Liz shone her torch around on the floor. 'Look, there's another one, and another! The FN .303 is what UNIT uses.'

'Yes, I know,' said the Doctor. 'But they haven't been down here for some time. I wonder if it could have been our elusive Major Barker?…'

'Well, anyway,' said Liz, 'let's find the point marked X on the map.' She took a step forward, but the Doctor suddenly grabbed her arm and pulled her back.

'That sand there,' he said, pointing, 'it's a little too smooth.' He looked around, found a small rock and threw it at the sand. The trellis-like man-trap sprung up from the smoothed sand, crushing the piece of rock. 'He came down here,' said the Doctor, 'got himself trapped in that thing and tried to shoot it out.'

Liz looked in horror at the man-trap. 'You think we can make peaceful contact with these monsters, Doctor?'

'I think we have got to,' he said. 'Now come on.'

They skirted round the man-trap and continued deeper in the cave. For the next thirty minutes they carefully followed the route sketched on Dr Quinn's map. It brought them into the huge cathedral-like cave where a little daylight came in from a distant opening to the outside world.

Liz said, 'What do you hope to find? I mean, what does the X mean on the map?'

But the Doctor pulled Liz sharply into a recess in the cave wall and signalled her to be silent. As they watched a reptile man appeared from one of the passages leading into the great cave. He went up to a huge rock and stood facing it. After a second or two his third eye glowed a brilliant red. The rock opened like a door and the reptile man went inside. The rock closed behind him. The Doctor could feel Liz quaking beside him.

'It was an upright lizard,' she said, 'a reptile!'

'It was also a man,' said the Doctor. 'An intelligent being.'

'But the reptiles were all stupid,' she said, as though she was desperately trying to believe it. 'Brains the size of kittens.'

'We only know about the reptiles whose fossils we have found,' said the Doctor. 'But what if for some reason the more intelligent reptiles hid themselves away in shelters under the Earth's crust?' As the Doctor talked he crossed over to the huge rock and inspected it. 'You see, there isn't even a crack to show how it opened.'

'Do we *want* to open it?' Liz asked.

'Of course we do,' said the Doctor. 'We must get inside there somehow.' He stood very still for a moment. 'Do you notice a slight breeze down here?'

'There's that opening up near the roof,' said Liz. 'Maybe it's windy outside now.'

The Doctor shook his head. 'It's a steady breeze, and it's moving in this direction.' The Doctor hurried off, Liz following. 'There you are,' he said, pleased with himself, 'an air-vent.'

Set in the wall of the cave was a circular tunnel about three feet high. The Doctor could feel air being sucked into it. He put his hand into the tunnel and felt the wall of the tunnel. It was perfectly smooth. 'I think this has just been made. What's more, it hasn't been drilled – it's been melted.'

'They've melted through this thickness of rock?' said Liz, hardly believing it possible.

'They certainly didn't cut their way through with a hammer and chisel,' said the Doctor. 'Now let's see where it takes us.

Hold on to my coat tails.'

The Doctor got on to all fours and started to climb into the tunnel. Liz scrambled along behind him. As they continued along the tunnel they could hear the humming of some electronic apparatus. The tunnel had a wide-angled bend in it, and as they passed the bend they could see a ring of light at the end of the tunnel.

'I'd rather have gone in by invitation,' said the Doctor, 'but at least this is a good second best.'

'Don't you think they'll be waiting for us at the other end?' called Liz.

'If they are,' said the Doctor, 'let me do the talking.'

Finally they reached the end of the tunnel. They emerged from it in a dark corner of the reptile men's giant shelter. The Doctor stood up and looked at the scene before him. They were in a huge, almost square cavern. All the walls and ceiling were made of sheet metal bolted together, like the hull of a ship. At one end was a huge pit with prison-like bars across its top, but the Doctor could not see what was kept in the pit. Elsewhere there were work-benches and tables. At one of these two reptile men were busy dismantling and inspecting an FN .303 rifle, clearly trying to understand how it worked. In a corner another two reptile men stood by a third which was lying on its back on a metal slab. Electrodes were attached to its head and feet. One of the reptile men in attendance pulled a big electrical switch set in the wall. The Doctor watched fascinated as the reptile man on the slab started to twitch.

'That's horrible,' said Liz, 'they're electrocuting it.'

'No,' the Doctor whispered, 'they are reviving it. Now watch.'

The reptile man on the slab continued to twitch for a full minute. Then the switch was turned off, and the electrodes were removed. The reptile man lay still for a moment, then slowly got up from the slab.

'*That's* what's happening to Dr Lawrence's current,' said the Doctor. 'I bet you they'll tell us they've just had another power loss when we get back.'

'*If* we get back,' Liz said.

But the Doctor's attention was already elsewhere, and he was quietly creeping away from the opening to the ventilation tunnel. Liz followed him. He was moving to a set of cages quite near to them. Major Barker was in the first cage, gripping the bars. A reptile man came up to the cage carrying a metal jug of water and a metal plate on which were a few dried pieces of some edible green leaf. The reptile man opened a little hatch in the cage and tried to hand in the jug and the plate.

'How long are you leaving me in here?' said Major Barker. 'They'll be coming after me, you know!'

The reptile man remained where he was, offering the food. Major Barker snatched the jug of water and threw it at the reptile man. 'I don't want your poison!'

The reptile man walked away. When he was some distance away, the Doctor went up quietly to the side of the cage. 'Major Barker,' he whispered.

Barker swung round. 'How did you get in here? Have you brought the troops?'

'No,' whispered the Doctor, 'we're alone. Is there any way we can get you out of there?'

'Not a chance,' said Major Barker. 'Some sort of electronic lock. Now listen,' he went on with all the authority of the victor rather than the vanquished, 'what you've got to do is to get yourselves out of here and tell the Brigadier what you've seen. These chaps are dangerous, you know.'

'Yes,' said the Doctor, 'I imagine they are.'

'I don't know whose side they're really on,' Major Barker went on, 'but there's something pretty big going on down here.

There's one thing I'm certain of – it's not good for England.'

'I quite agree,' said the Doctor.

'So you and your young lady had better chop-chop back to that Brigadier, and tell him to come down here with everything he's got. Bazookas, rockets, rifles, the lot. Got the idea?'

'If the Brigadier does that,' said Liz, 'you may get killed.'

'I'm a soldier, ma'am,' said the Major. 'Soldiers have to accept getting killed.'

'But you can only do it once,' said Liz.

'Under the circumstances,' said Major Barker, 'I don't think that's particularly funny.' He turned back to the Doctor. 'Everything understood?'

'Have they talked to you at all?' asked the Doctor.

'They keep asking me questions. Population of the Earth. What weapons we use. What foods we eat. Naturally I refused to answer. I tried to explain to them about the Geneva Convention concerning prisoners-of-war, but I don't think they understood.'

'No, I don't suppose they would,' said the Doctor. 'If they speak to you again, seem to co-operate with them a little, and see what you can find out about them.'

'I do not co-operate with the enemy,' said Major Barker. 'Still, if I do get a chance to find out anything, I shall bear your remarks in mind.' The Major looked down at himself. His clothes were torn and filthy, his hands grimy with cave dust. 'Sorry to have you see me in this condition, ma'am,' he said to Liz. 'I shall try to brush up a bit before we meet again.' He turned back to the Doctor. 'I really think you ought to get along now. No point in pushing one's luck.'

'But we can't leave you like this,' said Liz.

'No alternative, I'm afraid,' said the Major, and again turned to the Doctor. 'Remember now. Bring in the big guns, and let's get this sorted out once and for all.'

Two reptile men started to approach the cages. The Doctor quickly drew Liz away, and they sank back into the darkness of a corner. The reptile men went up to Major Barker.

'You have not eaten your food,' one of them said. 'We shall not offer food again, not until you answer our questions.'

'Then I shall starve to death,' shouted the Major.

The Doctor whispered close to Liz's ear. 'That's a very brave man, Liz. A fool. But a really brave man.'

The Doctor and Liz crept back to the opening of the air ventilation tunnel. Some minutes later they were back in the great cave and making their way back to the research centre.

14

Man from the Ministry

Dr Lawrence stood looking at the power dials in the cyclotron room. They all registered zero. At one time he would have been issuing orders to all the technicians and physicists around him, telling them to boost the nuclear reactor to get more power. But now he knew it was hopeless. Whatever force drained off the centre's vast electrical power output, it did it when it wanted to do it, and there was nothing Dr Lawrence could do to stop it.

'Reactors closed down safely,' said one of the technicians.

Dr Lawrence nodded. 'Just let me know when things get back to normal,' he said.

He left the cyclotron room and walked along the metal passageway to his office. He tried to remember how long he had been down in the research centre, five hundred feet below fresh air and sunshine. One week? Two? A month? Being a responsible man, he hadn't even taken an afternoon off-duty since the emergency started.

Once in his office, he closed the door, slumped into his chair behind the desk and put his head in his hands. He remembered how excited he was when he received the letter from the Ministry telling him that he had been appointed as Director of the Wenley Moor Research Centre. It was a job that many other scientists would envy. The pay was very good, but money wasn't the only attraction. He wanted to *do* something with his life, to

93

be remembered by future generations, like Faraday or Edison. Here, in this research centre, was the golden opportunity to do something that would be remembered, and it was all being ruined by forces he could not understand. His thoughts were interrupted by a tap on the door. Miss Travis, one of the young female technicians, entered.

'Excuse me, sir,' she said. 'I've just heard that Mr Masters is on his way here.'

'Who?' Dr Lawrence was so lost in thought that he couldn't remember any Mr Masters.

'The Permanent Under Secretary,' said Miss Travis.

Dr Lawrence was still confused. 'You mean he's left London to come here? When will he arrive?'

'He has arrived,' she said. 'He's coming down in the lift now. The guard at the top 'phoned down and I answered the 'phone.'

'Thank you for letting me know.' Dr Lawrence stood up, buttoned his jacket. 'Any chance you could rustle up some coffee for us?'

'I'll do what I can,' she said and left.

Dr Lawrence looked at himself in a wall mirror and straightened his tie. Then he cursed himself for behaving like this. Masters and he were at prep school together, had known each other since they were children. He had nothing to fear from Freddie Masters. On the contrary, perhaps Masters could sort out the whole awful mess. These thoughts were running through his head as the door was opened by a security guard and the Right Honourable Frederick Masters, M.P., entered. As always Masters was smiling, as though he had just won a General Election.

'Charles,' he said, advancing on Dr Lawrence with outstretched hand, 'I do hope you'll forgive my arriving unannounced like this.'

'You're most welcome,' said Dr Lawrence, remembering to add the friendly, 'Freddie.'

The smile on Masters's face faded for just a fraction of a second. 'I've rather dropped "Freddie" these days. "Frederick" seems to fit the image more, don't you think?' With this remark Masters made it clear that he was now rather important in the government, and Dr Lawrence was not.

'Yes, of course,' said Dr Lawrence. 'What can I do for you?'

Masters looked about the office, and ran a finger along a ledge which hadn't been dusted for some time. Then, as though he owned the place, he sat down in Dr Lawrence's chair behind the desk.

'What can you do for me?' he said, 'or isn't it rather what *I* can do for *you*?' He produced a perfectly white handkerchief, dusted the desk top before placing his elbows on it. 'I believe you are in terrible trouble.'

Dr Lawrence quaked. 'You mean with the government?'

'With everyone, dear boy,' said Masters. 'When I read your latest report, I just didn't know how I dare pass it on to the Minister.'

Dr Lawrence leant over his own desk and spoke earnestly. 'Something very strange is going on here, something outside of science as we know it…'

'You don't have to tell me,' Masters cut in with a wave of his immaculately manicured right hand. 'A dead pot-holer, another one gone mad; another technician killed by your own security officer with a blow on the head; and above all else, these extraordinary power losses.' He paused for effect, as though making a speech. 'You see, Charles, all these incidents might be acceptable to the government if at the same time there had been any progress in your work. But there has been no progress at all!' Then he put on the famous smile. 'Am I being beastly?'

'No,' said Dr Lawrence. 'Everything you say is true. In fact, since my last report the situation has worsened.'

'If that is possible,' said Masters. 'Do tell me more?'

Dr Lawrence knew there was no point in hiding anything. 'Major Barker, our security officer, was attacked by some person or persons unknown in the caves, and has since run away from the sick-bay. Dr Matthew Quinn has been murdered. Miss Dawson, one of our most important technicians, has become mentally unbalanced.'

Masters looked at Dr Lawrence for a full half-minute without speaking. 'Well, well,' he said at last, 'it just isn't your day, is it?'

'Look, Frederick,' said Dr Lawrence, lowering his voice. 'You've got to help me, for old time's sake. Is there any chance I could get out of this place?'

'You just get into that lift and press the button…'

Dr Lawrence cut in on Masters' facetious reply. 'I mean get another job somewhere.'

'With your qualifications,' said Masters, 'I should think that very easy. We have posts open in laboratories and research centres all over the country – for junior technicians.' He smiled again. 'You don't really want to be the first rat to leave a sinking ship, do you?'

'I know that if I remain here, and finally this place has to be written-off as a total loss, you people in the government will always hold the blame against me!'

'Come now,' said Masters. 'We aren't as beastly as that!' He paused again for effect. 'But you don't seem to have made much of a success of it all.'

Dr Lawrence sat down in one of the hard-backed chairs. He felt very tired and miserable. He knew he wouldn't get his own chair back while Masters remained here. 'What do you want me to do?' he asked.

'Some coffee would be nice,' said Masters.

'I've already ordered it.'

'And a little scientific progress would be even nicer,' said Masters. 'We sent you the Brigadier. Has he been of much help?'

Dr Lawrence shook his head. 'None at all, so far as I can see.'

The door was flung open and the Doctor and Liz entered, both grimy with cave dust. 'Dr Lawrence,' said the Doctor, 'have you just had a power failure?'

'We're always having power failures,' said Dr Lawrence.

'But the time of the last one,' said the Doctor urgently. 'It's most important.'

'At four twenty-two,' said Dr Lawrence. 'Now, if you don't mind, I'm trying to have a discussion with...'

But the Doctor ignored Dr Lawrence and turned to Liz. 'You see, it fits exactly. I checked my watch when we saw the reptile being de-hibernated.'

'May I ask who you are, sir?' said Masters with edge to his voice.

'You may indeed,' said the Doctor, and as he spoke Miss Travis entered with a tray of coffee for two. 'How terribly thoughtful of you, my dear,' he said to the startled girl technician, then turned to Dr Lawrence. 'Your people do look after us terribly well down here.' He took the tray from Miss Travis, set it on the desk in front of Masters and started to pour two cups of coffee. 'How many sugars, Liz?'

'One,' she said.

'To keep that figure of yours,' said the Doctor. 'Very wise.'

'That coffee,' said Dr Lawrence, 'was ordered for myself and the Permanent Under Secretary!'

'Really?' The Doctor was already sipping the cup he had poured for himself. 'Well, when he gets here, Miss Travis can make some more.'

'I'm already here,' said Masters.

The Doctor turned and looked down at Masters. 'My dear fellow, how appallingly thoughtless of me. Here, it's yours.'

Masters looked at the proffered cup. The Doctor's grimy finger-marks were all over it. 'I can wait,' he said. 'Why did you want to know the time of the last power loss?'

'Because we saw what happened to all your electricity,' said the Doctor. 'They use induction, you see, instead of cables.'

'*They?*' Masters was by now keenly interested.

'The reptiles,' said Liz. 'Like lizards.'

Masters drew back in his chair, not wishing to be contaminated by the madness of the two grimy people standing before him. 'Lizards who know how to use electricity?'

'It's quite logical,' said the Doctor. 'Humans sometimes use electricity to get muscles to work again.'

'Excuse me, sir,' said Miss Travis, who had been waiting by the open door, 'but should I get more coffee?'

'Yes,' said Dr Lawrence. 'A great amount of very black coffee.'

Miss Travis turned to go, and collided with the Brigadier as he entered. 'Mr Masters,' he said, going forward to shake hands. 'I've only just heard of your arrival. How are my reinforcements coming along?'

'They're not,' said Masters. 'That's one of the reasons I'm here. I really can't get the Regular Army to send support for you on the basis of a wild tale about monsters in caves.'

'But we have overwhelming evidence that there is something hostile in those caves,' said the Brigadier. 'The caves are vast, with a great many galleries and passageways. I need a lot of men to cover them completely.'

'Having covered them completely,' asked the Doctor, 'what do you intend to do?'

'Round up the saboteurs, or whoever they are,' said the

Brigadier, 'and bring them to justice.'

'We were hearing something about lizards,' said Masters, 'when you came in.' He turned to the Doctor. 'You did mention lizards, didn't you?'

'Miss Shaw used that term,' said the Doctor. 'I prefer to think of them as reptile men, or more accurately *homo reptilia*.'

'Doctor,' said the Brigadier, 'are you feeling all right?'

'A bit grubby,' said the Doctor. 'Otherwise I think I have all my senses about me, thank you.' He turned to Masters and Dr Lawrence. 'There is an entirely alien form of intelligent life living in those caves, gentlemen. It is highly dangerous. Most of them are still in a state of deep hibernation. Every time there is a power loss here it is because they are using your electricity to re-activate one of their own kind. Among other things, they have taken Major Barker prisoner.'

Masters, Dr Lawrence and the Brigadier stared at the Doctor in almost total disbelief. At last Masters spoke. 'Have you any evidence to support this extraordinary claim?'

'I have a witness,' said the Doctor. 'Miss Shaw here.'

'It's all true,' said Liz. 'We got into their place inside the caves. We talked to Major Barker.'

The Brigadier said, 'Then the sooner we get in there, with men and guns, the better.'

'I strongly advise against that,' said the Doctor. 'They have some idea about the power of our weapons, but we have no idea about theirs.'

'Quite honestly,' said Masters, 'I'm trying to do my best to cope with what you are saying, but I find it impossible to imagine a lizard armed with a sub-machine gun!'

'So do I,' said the Doctor. 'They are far too advanced for that sort of thing.' He turned to the Brigadier. 'I do implore you, Brigadier, don't invade those caves.'

'I'm sorry, Doctor,' the Brigadier said, 'but I have no

alternative. I was summoned here to help Dr Lawrence solve the problem of these terrible power losses. If you are right and some alien life-form is the cause of all this trouble, I must use what forces I have available to stop it.'

Dr Lawrence spoke up for the first time in minutes of silence. 'Doctor,' he said, 'can you suggest any other solution to our problem?'

'Indeed I can,' said the Doctor. 'I must go back there alone and try to make peace with these people.'

'*People?*' said Masters. 'You call lizards "people"?'

'It doesn't really matter what we call them,' said the Doctor. 'It's what arrangements we make with them that count.'

'But we are not going to make arrangements with reptile men,' said the Brigadier emphatically. He swung round to face Masters. 'You're sure there's no chance at all of getting those reinforcements?'

'No chance at all, old man,' said Masters. 'Not until we've got some proof that a real enemy exists, and not a couple of saboteurs.'

'I see,' said the Brigadier pulling back his shoulders. 'Then with the few men at my disposal, I shall invade the caves.'

'You may all be killed,' said the Doctor. 'Please leave it to me to go and talk to these creatures.'

The Brigadier shook his head. 'No, Doctor. This is a military matter. What's more, those caves are now strictly out-of-bounds to you or to any other civilian. I hope I make myself clear?'

'Absolutely clear,' said the Doctor.

'Then if you will excuse me, sir,' the Brigadier said to Masters. 'I must make my plans.' He left the office.

The Doctor sighed. 'Well, I suppose I had better make my plans, too,' he said, and turned to go.

'I'm afraid I still don't know quite who you are, sir,' said Masters.

The Doctor paused at the door and looked at Masters. 'I'm beginning to wonder myself,' he said, and left. Liz gave a quick smile to Dr Lawrence and Masters and hurried after the Doctor.

15

Attack and Counter-attack

It took the Brigadier a full ten minutes to get his men together to invade the caves. It took the Doctor only five minutes to drive Bessie from the research centre car park to the main mouth of the cave. By the time the Brigadier arrived, with two Jeeps and half-a-dozen soldiers, Bessie was standing there deserted, evidence that the Doctor had defied the Brigadier's instruction not to enter the caves.

'What are you going to do, sir?' asked Sergeant Hawkins.

The Brigadier bit his lip. 'I told him not to go in there. We shall have to press ahead just the same.'

'But if he tries talking to them,' said the Sergeant, 'and we roll up with guns, that isn't going to help him much, is it?'

'The Doctor is supposed to do what I tell him,' said the Brigadier, 'and so are you. Carry out the plan.'

'Yes, sir.' The Sergeant saluted, then ordered the other soldiers out of the Jeeps. As a precaution it was planned to leave one soldier at the mouth of the cave, and he would remain in telephone communication with the Brigadier and the other UNIT soldiers who entered the cave. The idea was that if none of the soldiers ever returned, at least the one soldier left at the mouth of the cave would know what happened to them. This could be helpful for any future attacks that might be planned. The lucky soldier, the one to be left at the mouth of the cave, was equipped with a field telephone. As the Brigadier and the soldiers advanced into the cave, they carried with them another field telephone and a drum of telephone wire which they paid out carefully as they penetrated the main passageway.

Sergeant Hawkins walked alongside the Brigadier, both flashing powerful torches. 'What do we do, sir, if we see something?' he asked.

'We fire first,' said the Brigadier, 'and ask questions afterwards.'

The Sergeant walked in silence for a while. Then he said: 'Sir?'

'Yes?'

'Do you really believe in these intelligent lizards?'

'Having been associated with the Doctor for some time now,' said the Brigadier, 'yes, I'm willing to believe in anything. But the idea of having peace-talks with them – that's another matter.'

The soldiers continued on their walk through the caves, guns at the ready. From time to time the Brigadier raised his hand and every man stood motionless as a statue, holding his breath. During these moments they all listened intently. All they heard was the drip-drip of distant water.

*

The Doctor crawled slowly on his hands and knees through the air ventilation-tunnel. As he approached the reptile men's shelter there was even more noise now. He emerged from its opening into the shelter, stood upright and tried to rub the grime from his hands. From the pit with the caged top there came a growling sound as from some very large animal that was kept down there. Another reptile man was being de-hibernated, which must have meant yet another power loss in the research centre. The Doctor had the impression that now there were even more reptile men going about their business. At least a dozen were standing around the bench where Barker's gun was now dismantled; the reptile men who had achieved this seemed to be explaining its parts to the onlookers.

The Doctor stepped from the darkened corner into a better-lit area. He could see Major Barker in his cage watching him in astonishment. Suddenly there was a commotion among the reptile men. One of them had spotted the Doctor, and was pointing him out to the others. The Doctor stepped forward and raised his voice. 'I have come to talk to you,' he said. 'I bring greetings from the other intelligent race that inhabits this planet.'

At first the reptile men were too surprised to do anything. Then three of them rushed at the Doctor, grabbed him violently and dragged him towards the prison cages. One of the trio looked at the cage's electronic lock; its third eye glowed for a second, and the lock sprang open. The cage door was pulled to one side, and the Doctor was pushed into the little caged cubicle. The cage door was pulled back, the lock refastened by a one-second glow from a reptilian third eye. Then the reptiles hurried away. The Doctor was in the next cage to Major Barker.

'A lot of good that did,' said the Major.

'It's a start,' said the Doctor. 'What's the food like here?'

'I have no idea,' said Major Barker. 'I only throw it back at them.'

Two reptile men, one old and the other younger, and both clearly in some authority, came forward to look at the new prisoner.

'You have come here,' said Okdel, 'of your own accord?'

'Of course,' said the Doctor. 'I think it's high time we all had a good talk.'

'We do not talk with apes,' said Morka.

'You used to,' said the Doctor. 'You used to talk to a man called Quinn, until you killed him.'

104

The old reptile man, Okdel, looked questioningly at Morka. 'You killed him?'

'He tried to hold me prisoner,' said Morka. He returned his attention to the Doctor. 'You wish to talk, ape. What about?'

'I want to help you,' said the Doctor.

'Just a minute,' Major Barker cut in. 'What do you think you're doing? I thought you were going to get help for *our* side!'

'I think their side may need it more,' said the Doctor.

'Do you realise that is treason, sir?' said the Major, then quoting from the law, '"Assisting a public enemy at war with the Queen"!' He turned to Okdel and Morka. 'This man is a traitor! If you, gentlemen, are true soldiers you will have nothing to do with him!'

'How do you wish to help us?' asked Okdel, ignoring the Major's outburst.

'I have come to warn you that men will shortly be entering these caves to look for you,' the Doctor said. 'If you do not attack them, they will not attack you. I want you to meet them in peace.'

'We do not "make peace" with apes,' said Morka. 'We exterminate apes.' He walked away purposefully.

The Doctor appealed to Okdel. 'Isn't it possible for both sides to live in peace?'

Okdel looked long and hard at the Doctor, then silently turned away.

'Come back!' called the Doctor. 'We have much to talk about.'

But Okdel had gone.

*

The Brigadier had stopped his men near where the water was dripping from the roof. Using their torches, he and Sergeant Hawkins looked at a map of the caves. The map was only partly complete, based on what passageways pot-holers had located and noted over the years. The Brigadier's plan was to inspect every inch of the caves by going down the passageways in an organised way.

'We shall proceed in that direction,' said the Brigadier, pointing to an opening in the cave wall.

'Yes, sir,' said the Sergeant. He called to the soldiers. 'This way, lads.'

They started to move off again, still paying out the telephone wire that led from their field telephone. Suddenly there was a cracking sound above them. The Brigadier and Hawkins shone their torches up on to the roof just ahead of them. A crack had appeared and was widening.

'Mind out!' called the Brigadier, but as he spoke a whole section of cave roof fell before them, blocking their way.

The passageway was choked with dust from the fall. As the dust started to settle, the Brigadier shone his torch ahead in the direction they had been going. The cave was completely blocked.

Sergeant Hawkins said, 'That looks like the end of that, sir.' He sounded almost pleased not to be able to go any deeper into the caves.

The Brigadier looked at the map again. 'We can go back down here,' he said, 'then work our way round again through some of these smaller passages.'

'About turn,' called Sergeant Hawkins. 'Back the way we came!'

The soldiers turned round to retreat down the main passageway. Then there was another cracking sound. Within a moment the cave roof further down the passageway had fallen in. Huge rocks barred their escape. They were completely trapped.

*

The Major glared at the Doctor from his cage. 'You had no right to tell them about the Brigadier's plan!'

The Doctor tried to reason with the Major. 'I simply want to prevent a massacre,' he said. 'Killing people isn't the only way to settle an argument.'

'It's the only way these creatures are likely to understand,' said the Major. 'Watch out, that vicious one's coming back.'

Morka came up to the cages. 'I wish to thank you for your warning,' he said to the Doctor. 'Your soldiers have all been killed. And now I shall kill you.' Morka focused his third eye on the Doctor. The eye started to pulsate with glowing redness.

'You will gain nothing by killing me,' said the Doctor, but already the power of Morka's radiation was having an effect on him. The Doctor felt as though he was being strangled, the air squeezed from his body. He fell to his knees. Intense pain raced through his arms and legs. He was just losing consciousness when he heard Okdel's voice.

'Stop!'

The pain continued through the Doctor's limbs. Morka had not heeded Okdel's order.

'Do not kill it,' said Okdel. 'It may be useful to us.'

Morka's third eye suddenly stopped glowing. 'What use can we make of the creature?'

'The other,' said Okdel, indicating Barker, 'has told us so little. I think this one is more intelligent. It can live for a little longer.'

'I have dealt with the apes sent to attack us,' said Morka. 'They are trapped in the caves.'

'You forget, there are now millions of this species,' said Okdel. 'They will send others to attack us.'

'Then we shall destroy them all,' said Morka. 'Ask your questions of this so-called intelligent ape, then I suggest you exterminate it.' Morka abruptly walked away.

Okdel stood looking at the Doctor. Slowly he asked, 'How many of your species now pollute our planet?'

'Over three thousand five hundred million,' said the Doctor, thinking it unwise at this moment to point out that Man was not his own species.

'That is impossible,' said Okdel. 'You give this enormous figure to frighten us.'

'I assure you,' the Doctor said, 'the figure is accurate. Since you were the rulers of Earth the apes, as you call Man, have multiplied time and time again.'

'We outnumber you by millions to one,' said Major Barker. 'So put that in your pipe and smoke it!'

'Do all carry these exploding sticks,' said Okdel, 'such as this ape had with him,' and he indicated Major Barker. 'Only soldiers,' said the Doctor.

'We *all* carry weapons,' cried Major Barker. 'Millions and millions of us!'

Okdel turned and looked at Barker. 'You lie. It will not help you.' He turned back to the Doctor. 'You say you wish to help us?'

'Yes,' said the Doctor. 'I can stop you from being destroyed.'

'We have studied your weapon. It is very primitive.'

'But you know nothing of the fighting power of the humans,' the Doctor said. 'You have only seen one rifle!'

'Be quiet!' said Barker. 'If you say another word about weapons, Doctor, I shall personally see that you are prosecuted under the Official Secrets Act!'

'What other weapons do you humans possess?' asked Okdel.

'Explosive shells that can penetrate armour-plating,' said the Doctor, 'bombs that can wipe out whole continents…'

The Doctor's words were choked as Barker put his hands through the bars dividing the two cages and grabbed the Doctor by the throat. 'I'll shut your mouth for you, you swine! You're a traitor! I'll stop you helping them!'

The Doctor tried to pull Major Barker's hands from his throat, but the Major had a steel-like grip. Okdel turned towards Major Barker, and his third eye started to pulsate. Barker suddenly fell away, a crumpled heap on the floor of his cage. The Doctor looked through the bars.

'Have you killed him?'

'No,' said Okdel. 'He will recover.'

The Doctor felt his bruised throat. 'Can't you let me out of here? I'm in no position to harm you, and I earnestly believe we must talk before it is too late.'

Okdel seemed to consider for a few moments. Then he looked down at the lock on the Doctor's cage door. His third eye pulsated, and the lock sprang open. 'Come with me,' he said. 'I have never talked with an ape before, but I realise that things have changed. Walk behind me.'

The Doctor followed close behind Okdel towards an inner room. Their route took them past the caged-over pit, and the Doctor stole a quick glance down into the pit. He caught a glimpse of the spiked back of a huge reptile, then hurried on after Okdel. The inner room also had walls of sheet metal riveted together. It was a small control-room with some devices for measuring the external temperature and air-condition. Okdel turned and stood facing the Doctor.

'If you attack me,' Okdel said, 'I shall destroy you instantly.'

'I have no intention of attacking you,' said the Doctor. 'I wish to help you.'

'What do you want to say?'

'First I need information,' said the Doctor. 'I want to know exactly why you have hidden yourselves in this shelter?'

'Quinn asked such questions,' said Okdel. 'It does not help us to provide you with information.'

'It may,' said the Doctor. 'Please tell me what happened?'

Okdel considered. Then he spoke again. 'A small planet, wandering through space, was attracted by the gravity of this planet. Our scientists said that when it swept by our planet it would cause great waves and winds. All life on the surface might be destroyed. So, we built these shelters; and, to save bringing food and water, we put ourselves into a form of hibernation. The return of the Earth's atmosphere, which would be drawn from the Earth for a short time, was to activate triggering devices on the surface that would automatically de-hibernate us. But somehow, something went wrong.'

'I think I can guess what it was,' said the Doctor. 'Did your planet have a moon?'

'Moon?' said Okdel, not understanding.

'You have given me the answer,' said the Doctor. 'You see,

that little planet you feared didn't sweep by Earth. It went into orbit around it. The atmosphere was never pulled away. It was the *return* of the atmosphere that was to activate your trigger devices, wasn't it?'

'Yes, its return.'

'How many of these shelters did you build?' asked the Doctor.

'I do not give you information,' said Okdel.

'I can only help if I know everything. How many are there?'

Again Okdel considered. 'Many thousands, all over the world. When we are ready we shall reactivate the others from this base.'

'That's understandable,' said the Doctor. 'But do you realise this could result in the most terrible war between two intelligent species in which both will be destroyed?'

'There is no alternative,' said Okdel.

'I think there is. In most of the world,' the Doctor said, 'the climate is very different from when it was your planet...'

'It remains *our* planet,' said Okdel.

'Nevertheless, over the last hundred million years or so the climate has changed,' said the Doctor. 'Your people thrive in hot climates, and there are still large areas in the world today very similar to the conditions in which you knew the planet, and these areas are hardly touched by Man. With your technology you could build cities in those parts of the world which Man has ignored.'

'We have cities,' said Okdel, 'great domed cities in valleys waiting for us to return.'

'No,' said the Doctor. 'This must be hard for you to understand, but there is no trace of your civilisation on this planet. The Earth's crust is always moving. You are fortunate that this shelter has not been crushed to pulp by some internal movement of the crust.'

Okdel seemed deeply affected to learn that his civilisation had completely vanished. 'Nothing of us has been found?'

'No,' said the Doctor. 'Only some fairly small versions of your animals – the lizard, the crocodile, and the snake.'

Okdel swayed slightly from one side to another, and from the depth of his throat there came a gentle whining sound. The Doctor thought this must be the reptile man's way of showing grief. Then a single drop of liquid slid from one of Okdel's eyes. The old reptile man was crying.

'I am very sorry,' said the Doctor. 'It must be sad to realise that you are so completely forgotten.'

Okdel stopped swaying. He did nothing to conceal the single tear, which had left a glistening path down the scales of his face. 'These areas of which you speak,' said Okdel at last. 'Would your people agree to this?'

'They are not my people,' said the Doctor, 'but I think they might listen to me. First you must release the men who are trapped in the caves. This will help me to convince the humans that you do not intend to harm them.'

'These apes have only shown hostility to us,' said Okdel. 'The other in the cage tried to hurt my friend, Morka.'

'You have only shown hostility to the humans,' said the Doctor, 'by releasing your fighting animals in the caves. But someone must make the first move towards peace.'

'We are a peace-loving species,' said Okdel. 'But it is difficult for us to think of apes as equals.'

'There are some hard pills to swallow,' said the Doctor, 'and one of them is that the apes have grown up.'

'If your plan is acceptable to the other species,' said Okdel, 'it would be understood that we are the superior race?'

'I am sure that the humans could learn to treat you with great respect,' said the Doctor. 'But these days people don't talk about superior and inferior races. Everyone is equal.'

'Every one of the humans is equal,' said Okdel. 'But we must be respected.'

'I would certainly try to arrange that,' said the Doctor.

'Good. Then I shall release the apes in the cave.' Okdel's third eye started to glow very gently.

*

The Brigadier and his men sat slumped against the wall of the cave. The dust from the roof falls has completely settled now, so that they were not choking from it. But with a total blockage at each end of the passageway no air was able to get in or out. The Brigadier looked up and down the passageway, and tried to make a mental calculation as to the number of cubic feet of air they had to breathe, and then to equate that figure with the number of men. If they were lucky, they had another three or four hours but no more. Sergeant Hawkins came over to the Brigadier and slumped down beside him.

'What about getting the lads to try to shift the rocks again?' said Hawkins.

The Brigadier shook his head. They had already tried that, and found the rocks impossibly heavy to move. 'The less the physical activity,' said the Brigadier, 'the longer our oxygen is going to last. Try the telephone again.'

'Yes, sir.' Sergeant Hawkins scrambled over to the field telephone, and cranked the handle. He listened. The line was dead. 'The lead must have been cut by the rock fall,' he told the Brigadier. 'There isn't a sound.'

The Brigadier stood up. 'Remain seated, everyone,' he said. 'It's a soldier's job to *do* things, not to sit on his backside. But the situation is rather against us. If we try heaving at those rocks we shall run out of oxygen in no time. The telephone's been cut. But if we remain here, quietly, not even talking, we can last out a very long time.' He knew this was a lie, but he had to give his soldiers some hope. 'Eventually, our non-return is going to be noted by the people at the research centre. There's a man from the Ministry of Defence there at the moment. He's bound to take action. Other troops will be sent in to dig us out. Understood?'

There was a murmur of understanding from the soldiers. The Brigadier sat down again. Then he noticed the scratching sound coming from one end of their walled-in section of passageway. He flashed his torch in the direction of the sound. Private Robins was crouched against the cave wall apparently scratching a stone against the wall. The Brigadier quietly signalled to Hawkins to follow, then went down the passageway towards Robins. 'Something up, Robins?' he said.

Robins did not reply. The Brigadier came up behind Robins and flashed his torch on to the wall where Robins was scratching with the stone. Etched into the wall of the cave were crude drawings of animals and what might be men. Hawkins had come up behind the Brigadier. 'Robins,' said Hawkins, 'pull yourself together, lad!' Robins took no notice and continued with his crude wall drawings.

'Leave him alone,' said the Brigadier.

There was a sudden rumble at the other end of the area in which they were trapped. 'Sir,' said Hawkins, 'down there – more of the roof falling in!'

The Brigadier and Sergeant Hawkins swung their powerful torches in the direction of the increasing sound. 'I don't believe it,' said Hawkins. 'I don't believe it!'

As they watched the great mass of rocks and boulders that blocked their escape rose up from the floor of the cave, all neatly going back exactly into position to reform the cave roof.

'I quite agree with you,' said the Brigadier. 'I don't believe it either, but let's get out of here while we've got the chance.'

'What about Robins, sir?'

'Two of you men,' called the Brigadier, 'come and give

Robins a hand.'

Two soldiers sprang forward and helped Robins to his feet.

'Now then, men,' shouted the Brigadier, 'back down the passageway to base. And sharp about it!'

Grinning, all the men scrambled to their feet and started moving off down the passageway.

*

Okdel's third eye stopped pulsating. He turned to the Doctor. 'The apes in the cave have been released.'

'Thank you,' said the Doctor. 'Are any of them hurt?'

'No,' said Okdel. 'They are all unharmed.'

'Good. Now you must allow me to return, and I shall tell the humans what you have done.'

Morka entered and stood himself directly in front of Okdel. 'Why have you released the humans?'

Okdel said, 'I have decided it is possible for the two species to live together on this planet.'

'This planet is ours!' Morka stormed.

'Not exclusively,' said the Doctor.

'We are the masters of our planet by birthright,' said Morka. 'All other species are inferior.'

'This other species,' said Okdel, 'has developed its own civilisation. We must accept them, and hope that they will accept us.'

'They are savages,' said Morka. 'See this wound in my leg? This is the work of these animals.'

'That was a mistake,' said Okdel. 'These are intelligent beings. We can reason with them.'

'If they are so intelligent,' Morka said, 'they can serve us as slaves. Either they accept that, or we destroy them!'

'I shall decide what is to become of the humans,' said Okdel. 'Not you. Now leave me.'

For a moment Morka's third eye glowed in uncontrollable

rage, and the Doctor felt a twinge of pain across his own forehead. Then Morka turned and left the inner room.

*

As Morka left the inner room, his thin body quivered with rage. In the far corner the scientist K'to was completing the de-hibernation of yet another reptile man. Morka crossed over to K'to.

'Okdel speaks of sharing our planet with apes,' he said.

'And your opinion?' asked K'to carefully.

'We should kill them all.'

K'to said, 'Since our time they have mutated and developed far beyond anything we ever expected. That is obvious from the two specimens we have caught.'

'They are still mammals,' said Morka, 'the lowest form of life!'

'Okdel is the leader of this shelter,' said K'to. 'Perhaps when the other shelters have been found and re-activated, there will be different ideas among the other leaders.'

But Morka was not really listening. 'I trapped the humans in the caves, and Okdel has released them. Now I shall try to destroy them!'

'It is dangerous to disobey Okdel,' said K'to.

Morka raised a hand. 'Silence!' His third eye started to pulsate as he concentrated. K'to remained watching Morka, wondering what was going on in his mind, and what effect it was having on the humans in the caves.

*

The UNIT soldiers came along the passageway, all in good spirits now. One or two were whistling a familiar tune. The first one to start behaving strangely was Sergeant Hawkins. He stopped suddenly and blinked. The Brigadier hurried up beside him.

'What's the matter, Sergeant?'

116

'Don't know, sir. I just felt a bit peculiar for a moment.' Hawkins shook his head, then continued to walk forward. From behind them there was a sudden scream. Both Hawkins and the Brigadier whirled round to see Robins fighting desperately with the two soldiers who had been helping him.

'Robins!' The Brigadier doubled back to the soldier. 'We're getting you back to base as quickly as possible, Robins. Now pull yourself together!'

Robins glared at the Brigadier, his eyes wild with fear. Then, using enormous strength, he broke free from the two soldiers on either side of him and darted off down one of the smaller tunnels. The Brigadier rushed after him. 'Robins,' he called, 'I've no idea where this goes. You'll get yourself lost.'

The tunnel was quite short. It opened up into a dome-roofed cave. There was a wide ledge where the tunnel came out, then a black chasm. As the Brigadier came out on to the ledge, his torch picked up Robins perched on the edge of the ledge. Sergeant Hawkins came up behind the Brigadier.

'What do we do now, sir?' Hawkins asked.

'Pray, I should think,' said the Brigadier. He called softly to Robins. 'Robins, take a step backwards.'

They waited to see if Robins would respond. Robins lifted one foot, held it poised a moment, then swung it back from the chasm.

'Good man,' said the Brigadier. 'Now bring the other leg one step backwards.'

Again they had to wait to see how Robins would react. He lifted his other leg, held it poised, then stepped back. He was now no longer right on the edge of the chasm.

'Now then, Robins,' said the Brigadier, in the same quiet voice. 'Eyes right, and about turn!'

Robins carried out the order as though he were on the parade ground.

'That's very good going,' said the Brigadier. 'Now I want you to march, shoulders back, towards me.'

Like a sleep-walker, Robins began to march very slowly towards the Brigadier. 'He's going to be all right,' whispered Sergeant Hawkins. 'You've pulled him through it, sir.'

'A bit more towards me,' said the Brigadier, and Robins slightly altered his direction to take himself directly to the Brigadier. As Robins came up close the Brigadier said, 'Good man! Now you're safe, and you're with friends.'

Robins smiled at the Brigadier. Then some strange wild look flashed in his eyes. 'Grab him,' shouted the Brigadier, and Sergeant Hawkins lunged forward. Robins recoiled backwards in sudden panic, then turned and ran straight for the chasm. His body hurtled into the darkness. The Brigadier and Hawkins rushed to the edge and looked down. A long-drawn-out scream came up to them, a scream that never seemed to end. The scream went on, fading further and further into the distance, as Robins plummeted into the bowels of the Earth. The Brigadier and the Sergeant remained standing where they were for some time. Then the Brigadier moved away from the chasm. 'There's nothing we can do for him, Sergeant. We'd better press on.'

Sadly the two men made their way back to the waiting soldiers.

*

Morka's third eye stopped pulsating.

'What have you done?' asked K'to.

'Killed one of them,' said Morka. 'They have moved out of range. I can only control the weakest.'

'Or the least mutated,' said K'to.

'There are other ways to kill apes,' said Morka. 'I have released one of our fighting animals into the caves. Later I shall release all our animals to destroy the humans.'

'Okdel will stop you,' said K'to. 'In any case if it is true that so many apes now pollute our planet, our fighting animals will be of little use against them.'

Morka found this a terrible thought. 'We cannot let the apes over-run us! They are vermin!'

'I agree,' said K'to. 'But our fighting animals alone cannot now destroy them.'

Morka looked more closely at K'to. 'I think you are really a friend of mine,' he told the scientist. 'Before now, I thought you had no opinions, no feelings.'

'Because I am a man of science,' K'to said, 'does not mean that I lack feelings and passions. I have no wish to share the world with furry creatures. They are unclean. Insects sometimes live in their fur. They disgust me.'

'Do you see some solution to our problem?' Morka asked. 'There are few of us but millions of them.'

K'to went to a metal cupboard, opened it and brought out a sealed canister. 'In our time you worked in the domed city,' he said. 'You were not a farmer, so there were things you did not know. As a scientist I had to assist our farmers. When the apes raided their crops, the substance in this canister was used. It is lethal.'

'Can we be sure that it will work on apes as they are now?' asked Morka.

'Fortunately,' said K'to, 'we can conduct an experiment.' He turned and looked towards the prisoner cages. Major Barker was just recovering consciousness, and was rubbing his head.

'Kill him with this substance?' said Morka, not yet fully understanding. 'Killing them one at a time will not help us.'

'We shall not kill him,' said K'to. 'We shall let him free, and he will kill all the others for us.'

*

The Brigadier and the UNIT soldiers were making slow progress on their way out of the caves. Every foot of the field telephone cable had to be wound back on to the drum, and this slowed them down.

'We couldn't just leave the cable, could we, sir?' asked Sergeant Hawkins.

'Government property,' said the Brigadier.

'But hanging about like this, sir,' Hawkins persisted. 'We could get trapped again by a roof-fall.'

'If we are trapped again,' said the Brigadier, 'that is something I could explain to my superiors. But if I lose one foot of that wretched telephone cable, there will be an investigation into the waste of public money.'

The two soldiers winding the cable back on to the drum worked as fast as they could, and the little group of UNIT men moved forward down the passageway. Then Sergeant Hawkins stopped, and pointed his torch on to the cave floor.

'Look, sir,' he said. 'I'm sure that wasn't here before.'

The Brigadier looked down at a perfect footprint of one of the reptile fighting animals. He felt very worried about the sight of it. 'We may have to forget that wretched telephone cable after all,' he told the Sergeant.

Even as the Brigadier spoke, his words were drowned by the roar of the fighting animal which had appeared a couple of hundred feet down the passageway. Its mouth had huge pointed teeth, bared now as it advanced towards the soldiers. To the animal, these humans were food.

'Shoot for the head!' shouted the Brigadier, himself taking cover behind an outcrop of rock. All the soldiers dived for the sides of the passageway. 'Fire now!'

The soldiers opened up with a rain of bullets at the monster. The Brigadier could see bullet holes appearing in the monster's thick scaly hide, but even so the monster continued towards the soldiers, roaring and baring its long pointed teeth.

'We need explosive bullets for this,' said Hawkins, as he

fired round after round at the oncoming monster.

The Brigadier saw one of the soldiers reach for a hand grenade to throw. 'No grenades,' he shouted. 'You fool – you'll bring the roof down on top of us!'

All at once the monster stopped in its advance. 'Hold your fire,' called the Brigadier. 'And put out the torches.' They all snapped off their torches. There was total darkness. Through the darkness came the heavy breathing of the monster. 'The torches were attracting it,' said the Brigadier, just loud enough for everyone in the confined space to hear.

'But we can't see how close it is now, sir,' said Sergeant Hawkins. 'It's got the advantage.'

'We can listen,' said the Brigadier.

The heavy breathing continued. Then they heard the monster move its feet. 'I think it's going away,' said the Brigadier. 'Keep those torches turned off until we can't hear it.'

The men waited, hardly daring to move. Eventually there was no sound of the monster. The Brigadier switched on his torch. The passageway ahead was empty. He straightened up. 'Torches on,' he said, and the other men switched on their torches. 'Now let's get out of these caves as quickly as we can.'

'What about the cable, sir?' said Sergeant Hawkins.

'That's right,' said the Brigadier, 'what about it?' He grinned at the Sergeant. 'For once, let's forget about government property and look after our own necks!'

The Brigadier and the soldiers ran as fast as they could down the passageway towards freedom.

*

Major Barker found himself lying on his back on the floor of the great cathedral-like cave. Daylight filtered in from the opening up near the roof of the cave. He sat up and tried to remember what had happened. Everything was rather confused. He could remember the man-trap that caught him by the ankles, and those horrible reptile faces advancing on him. Then he was a prisoner for some time, held in a cage like an animal. There was another prisoner, that Doctor fellow, but one of the reptiles took him away. Now his memory started to come back. The Doctor had been a traitor, and had wanted to help these lizards.

Perhaps they had taken the Doctor away to kill him. No decent person liked traitors. But these were lizards, not 'persons'. Major Barker rubbed his head. It was all very strange.

His arm itched. He pulled up the sleeve of his jacket to scratch his arm. He looked at the flesh of his forearm, saw a little cut in the flesh. How had he been cut there? He could not remember. Anyway, it was a very tiny wound, nothing to worry about. But it itched badly, and he scratched at it viciously. Then he looked at the blood on his fingers from the wound. Perhaps best not to scratch it, he thought. His hands and fingers were filthy with cave dust, and he might infect the wound. He steeled himself not to feel the itch, and to leave his arm alone.

He stood up and looked about himself. So, he thought, he had somehow escaped. The trouble was, he couldn't *remember* escaping. Still, the mind can play strange tricks. Obviously he must have escaped or he would not be in this cave now, a free man. Somehow in his escape he must have banged his head against a rock, and that's why he was lying unconscious on the cave floor. All he had to do now was to find his way out of the caves, and obviously the quickest way was to climb up to that little circle of daylight near the roof.

He started to move off when his foot kicked something. For a ghastly moment he expected a man-trap to grab his ankles. But nothing happened. He looked down, saw his rifle lying on the floor. He picked it up, checked that it still worked. Then he started to climb up the rocks leading to the daylight.

From a dark recess between rocks, the reptile scientist K'to watched Major Barker with considerable interest. Once Major

Barker had reached the circle of daylight, K'to moved towards the great rock, pulsated his third eye and opened the rock. He went inside, and the rock closed behind him.

*

The Doctor was alone in the inner room, where Okdel had left him. The moment Okdel left, the Doctor tried the door, only to find Okdel had locked it. The Doctor interested himself in a screen in the wall. There were a number of dials and buttons set in the wall immediately under the screen, and experimentally the Doctor tried some of these controls. Instantly the screen lit up showing a map of Earth before the Great Continental Drift. He touched the controls again. The map vanished from the screen and was replaced by an aerial view of a domed city. Then the door opened and Okdel entered, carrying a metal canister.

'You must have had a great civilisation,' said the Doctor, indicating the picture of the city on the screen.

Okdel ignored the Doctor's remark. 'I have spoken to the others of your plan,' he said. 'Some wish to live in peace with the humans, and others do not. But without my knowing, something has happened which may change all our plans. The other prisoner has been released.'

'I'm very pleased to hear that,' said the Doctor.

Okdel raised a scaly hand to silence the Doctor. 'No, you will not be pleased. He has been infected with a deadly virus which may destroy all his species.' Okdel paused, and swayed a little from side to side. 'It is not my doing. I am sorry.'

'What will this virus do?' asked the Doctor.

'I saw it used against the apes,' said Okdel. 'It was very cruel. First it causes a surge of energy which burns up the body's resources. With some, death follows almost immediately, with great pain. With others, the afflicted ones wander mindlessly over great distances, infecting all others. The disease spreads with incredible speed.'

'Is there an antidote?' said the Doctor. 'Any cure?'

'I do not know,' said Okdel. 'Since it only affected the apes, we had no need to develop an antidote. That is why I have brought you this.' He offered the canister to the Doctor. 'Your civilisation has scientists, has it?'

'Yes,' said the Doctor.

'The virus is in this substance. Take it to your scientists, ask them to develop an antidote.'

The Doctor took the canister, holding it very carefully. 'That might take weeks.'

'Of course,' said Okdel. 'I fear many of the human species will die. That cannot now be avoided. But with this substance, you have a slight chance.' Okdel turned to the door and opened it again. 'Now I shall release you. You must come with me.'

'What about your friends who have released this virus?' the Doctor said, as he followed Okdel out of the inner room.

'I hope they will understand why I have released you,' Okdel said, leading the Doctor towards the door to another inner room. 'If they do not, they will be very angry.'

Okdel stopped at the door to the other inner room. He looked at the lock, and for a second his third eye glowed red. The lock clicked, and the door opened by itself. 'Go through there,' said Okdel. 'Other doors will open as you go forward. Then you will find yourself outside this shelter and in a great cave. From there you must find your own way.'

'Thank you,' said the Doctor. 'I hope that we shall meet again soon.'

Okdel said nothing. The Doctor entered the inner room, and the door closed soundlessly behind him. Then another door in front of him opened, just as Okdel had promised.

*

Okdel stood by the door for some minutes after the Doctor had gone. He felt very old. It was still so difficult for him to accept that up on ground-level nothing remained of his civilisation. He thought about these hot arid places which the Doctor had said the humans might set aside for the reptile people to live in – the Sahara, Arabia, Central Australia. None of these names meant anything to Okdel. He felt too old and tired to think of building new domed cities.

Slowly he walked back to the inner room where he had talked with the Doctor. The picture of a domed city was still on the screen. He went up to the screen and touched a control. A moving picture appeared showing his people's first attempt at flight. The flying-machine was very small and only carried two young reptile men. The picture cut to a crowd waving to the brave young aviators. All this had happened when Okdel was young. Later their flying-machines were developed to carry hundreds of passengers at a time. He turned another control to bring up a picture of more personal memories. It showed himself as a young reptile man winning a race. His limbs were far too old and fragile to race now. The picture changed, and there was an ape in a cage in Okdel's garden. His friends had thought him very strange to keep an ape as a pet, but Okdel had taken a liking to the animal. The ape jumped about the cave, then picked up a slate and a pencil and started to make a crude drawing of animals and reptile men. This had always fascinated Okdel, the fact that an animal could draw pictures. He wished that he had been able to bring his pet ape with him into the shelter.

Suddenly he was aware that he was not alone. He switched off the screen and turned round. Morka and K'to had entered the room and were standing side by side. Okdel knew what was going to happen.

'Where is the other human?' said Morka.

'I have released him,' said Okdel. 'I gave him the substance so that the humans can find an antidote.'

'You want them to destroy us?' said Morka.

'They will not destroy us,' said Okdel, 'and we need not destroy them. There are places on the planet where our species can continue to live.'

'They will not allow us to live,' said K'to. 'The ape Quinn told us how the humans are killing off all other species on the planet. They are mammals, yet they exterminate other mammals. What chance have we while these humans exist?'

'If we fight them,' said Okdel, 'they will win.'

'Never!' said Morka. 'The lethal substance could kill them all if you had not interfered.'

Okdel sensed that his life was almost at an end. He said what was truly in his mind. 'The planet is cooler, the atmosphere thinner, than in our day. All our civilisation is destroyed. Perhaps it is a mistake even to think of starting again.'

'You propose that vermin shall take our world?' said Morka.

'They have already taken it,' said Okdel. 'We can but hope for the smallest share.'

'You have betrayed us,' said Morka. He turned to K'to. 'Kill him now!'

Okdel saw the two third eyes before him turn to a brilliant red. The pain raced through his old limbs. For a moment he remembered himself as a tiny reptile baby, breaking out from its egg. Then his mind went blank and he was dead.

16

The Itch

The Right Honourable Frederick Masters presided over the meeting from what was normally Dr Lawrence's chair behind the desk. Dr Lawrence had to occupy one of the hard-backed chairs, and sat next to Liz. On the other side of Liz was Major Barker and the Brigadier. She noticed how Major Barker was sweating profusely, and kept scratching at his arm.

'I tell you,' said Barker, 'that Doctor is a traitor! He's co-operating with them.'

'Co-operating with reptile men,' said Masters, turning to the Brigadier. 'Do you believe in these creatures?'

Liz couldn't stop herself answering for the Brigadier. 'Mr Masters, I've seen them. Everything Major Barker says is true – except about the Doctor being a traitor.'

Major Barker swung round to face Liz. 'You weren't there when he started to make deals with them!' He scratched furiously at his arm, then tried to stop himself.

'If I may make a point,' said Dr Lawrence, 'I find this all scientifically impossible. In any case, the point at issue is these power losses!'

'I agree,' said Masters, 'but I really cannot prepare a report for the government on the basis of what I've heard so far.'

Major Barker exploded. 'There's no time for reports, sir! We must blow up every entrance to those caves before they over-run us.'

'I agree,' said Dr Lawrence, 'that would probably be very sensible.'

'It wouldn't stop your power losses,' Liz said. 'And you mustn't blow up the entrances while the Doctor is still down there.'

Masters turned to the Brigadier. 'I believe you told your Doctor that the caves were out-of-bounds to him – is that correct?'

The Brigadier mumbled over his words. 'Well, yes, er, I did advise him to keep clear of the caves…'

'Advice which he ignored?' said Masters, cutting in.

'He's a very self-willed fellow,' said the Brigadier.

'A traitor, if you ask me!' shouted Major Barker.

Masters swung round to face Barker. 'I didn't ask you, and I'd be glad if you would remember that *I* am chairing this meeting. And another thing, Major Barker: stop scratching yourself. It annoys me.'

Major Barker stopped scratching himself instantly, shocked by the way he had been spoken to. Liz looked from him to Masters. Masters didn't look at all well. Beads of perspiration stood out on his forehead.

'Now then,' said Masters, who seemed to be losing his grip of the meeting, 'where had we got to?'

'We have to rescue the Doctor,' said Liz, taking the opportunity to make her point. 'He's still in the caves.'

The Brigadier said, 'Well, I can't mount a proper rescue until I get an adequate number of troops and equipment.'

'I don't think a rescue is really included on our agenda,' said Masters. 'The Doctor defied the Brigadier's ban, and went into the caves of his own free will.'

Liz protested, 'That doesn't mean you can leave him there!'

'How thoughtful of you, Liz!' The Doctor's voice boomed from the open door. Everyone swung round to see the Doctor as he entered. He carried in his hand the metal canister. 'Now I want you all to move away from Major Barker.' He turned to Barker with a smile. 'Sorry to be treating you like a leper, old man, but – well, that is what you are for the time being.'

Major Barker rose slowly, quivering with rage. His face had gone beetroot. Liz thought one of the veins in his temples might burst at any moment. 'You blackguard,' he said to the Doctor. 'You filthy traitor! I'm placing you under arrest.'

Major Barker moved to grab the Doctor, but the Doctor quickly sidestepped out of Barker's way. 'Listen to me, Major,' he said, 'you're an ill man. You have a terrible infection.'

'What are you talking about?' Barker demanded. 'You, sir, are a criminal of the worst order. I've told them all about you. I'm taking you into custody, and I suggest that you come quietly.' The Major crossed to the Doctor and tried to grip his arm.

The Doctor stepped back again. 'I warn you, Major, you're an ill man. And above all, you mustn't touch anyone…'

The Major staggered, then lunged forward at the Doctor. The Doctor backed as far as he could, until his back was against the wall. Suddenly the Major stopped in his advance. He closed his eyes for a moment, then suddenly grabbed at his own wrist as though it was burning. 'My arm,' he said, his voice hardly audible, 'it's killing me.' He staggered again, and sank to his knees, then pulled up his jacket and shirt sleeve. A huge bright red mark stood out on his arm where previously there had been the tiny wound. 'It's festering,' he gasped, 'I'll lose my arm. The pain – it's too much…' He suddenly collapsed in a faint.

The Doctor knelt down and examined the mark on Barker's arm. Meanwhile Dr Lawrence had lifted his internal 'phone and was telling Dr Meredith to hurry along here from the sick-bay. The Brigadier and Masters came and looked down at the bright red mark on Barker's arm.

'What's the matter with him?' said Masters.

'He's being used as a carrier,' said the Doctor. 'I believe the skin under that mark is filled with an infectious virus.'

'No wonder he kept scratching his arm,' said Masters, and pulled out a spotless white handkerchief and mopped his brow. 'Charles,' he said to Dr Lawrence, 'can you turn up the air-conditioning in here a bit? It's terribly warm.'

Dr Lawrence adjusted the air-conditioning. Cold air started to pump in through grilles near the ceiling. 'Dr Meredith will be here in a moment,' he said. He turned to the Doctor. 'What's this about you making a deal with lizards?'

'There is a life-form in a special shelter in the caves,' the Doctor said. 'It is intelligent. But whatever Major Barker has told you, things have since changed. This canister contains enough poison to wipe out the entire human race. This place must be put into strict quarantine, and I need a fully equipped laboratory in order to find an antidote for what's in this canister.'

'You'll bring the Centre to a standstill,' said Dr Lawrence.

'And those "lizards" will bring Mankind to a standstill,' said the Doctor.

Dr Meredith hurried in. 'You wanted me, sir?'

Dr Lawrence indicated Barker on the floor. 'Major Barker's collapsed, probably through exhaustion.'

Dr Meredith looked down at Barker. 'Does anyone know how he got that mark on his arm?'

'A lizard bit him,' said Masters, and gave a silly laugh.

'Perhaps one of you gentlemen could help me get him to the sick-bay,' said Dr Meredith.

'Allow me,' said the Brigadier, and knelt down to raise up Major Barker.

'No one should touch him,' said the Doctor. 'That's exactly what they want us to do.'

The Brigadier looked up from the floor. 'Doctor, we can't be sure of that, and in any case we can't leave the poor man lying here. Ready, Dr Meredith?'

Together, Dr Meredith and the Brigadier lifted Major Barker between them and carried him out of the office.

'If you don't mind,' said Masters, 'we'll adjourn the meeting for a few minutes. I suppose your sick-bay has got aspirins and that sort of thing. I'm so busy, I hardly had any sleep last night. I'll be back shortly.' He followed Dr Meredith and the Brigadier out of the office.

'Now,' said the Doctor to Dr Lawrence, 'I'm going to need the full use of your laboratory, and in particular I'll need an electron microscope.'

'That's all very interesting,' said Dr Lawrence scathingly, 'but I really don't understand why.'

'Then I had better try to explain,' said the Doctor. He carefully took Dr Lawrence through the whole story of his encounter with the reptile men. It was clear from Dr Lawrence's face that at first he thought the Doctor was out of his mind. But as the Doctor progressed with his story, some of the time supported by Liz's own account of what she had seen, Dr Lawrence gradually became convinced. Halfway through the story, Masters returned, so the Doctor had to repeat a lot of what he had already told Dr Lawrence. Towards the tail-end the Brigadier reappeared.

When the Doctor had finished, Dr Lawrence was the first to speak: 'At least that exonerates me,' he said smugly.

'Is that your only reaction,' said the Doctor, 'to the existence of an entirely separate life-form in the caves – that it exonerates *you*?'

'My task is to make this research centre operate efficiently,' said Dr Lawrence.

'I must say,' said Masters to the Doctor, 'you have presented us with a rather considerable problem. There's a government meeting I have to attend later today in London. The only thing I can recommend is that this centre be closed.'

Dr Lawrence was crestfallen. 'But the trouble has nothing to do with this centre! You've just heard the Doctor explain that!'

'The objective fact is,' said Masters, 'that we cannot make this place work, at least not until these animals have been exterminated.'

'Talking of extermination,' said the Doctor, trying to get the conversation back to the most immediate problem, 'the way things are going *you* are likely to be exterminated, not the reptile men.' He turned to the Brigadier. 'How's Major Barker now?'

'He's remained in the coma,' said the Brigadier. 'Dr Meredith's packed him off to the cottage hospital.'

The Doctor shot up out of his chair. '*What?* That's the worst thing he could have done. I said this whole centre should be in quarantine! We need to get that man back here immediately.'

'You don't *really* believe in this virus thing, do you?' asked Masters.

'Of course I do,' said the Doctor. 'Why do you think they released Major Barker?'

The Brigadier said, 'He told us how he fought his way out of the reptile place. That was before you arrived.'

'Whatever he told you, it isn't true,' said the Doctor. 'Liz, we've got to get to that hospital. We must warn them of what's happened.'

Liz got up to go.

'Hold on, Doctor,' said the Brigadier. 'If you really think we've done the wrong thing, I'd better go with you.'

'Thank you,' said the Doctor, and turned again to Liz. 'Then you stay here and try to get an electron microscope for me. Come on, Brigadier, we haven't a moment to lose.'

The Doctor and the Brigadier hurried out.

'May I use the 'phone?' Liz asked.

'Help yourself,' said Dr Lawrence, despair in his voice. 'I'll see that our laboratory is made clear for you.'

Masters got up, a little unsteadily, Liz thought, and put his papers back into his black ministerial brief-case. 'I'll have to get back to London.'

'I'll see you to the lift,' said Dr Lawrence. 'Are you sure you're fit to travel? You don't look too well.'

'All I need is a good night's sleep,' said Masters. 'Nice to have met you, Miss Shaw. I hope we meet again sometime under more pleasant circumstances.'

Masters reached out to shake hands with Liz. Liz noticed how hot and clammy his hand was. Then she turned her attention to the telephone, to find someone who could quickly provide the Doctor with the special equipment he now needed.

17

Epidemic

The Brigadier kept his foot well down on the Jeep's accelerator as it took a bend on the moorland road. Beside him the Doctor clung on to a grab-handle, his curly hair billowing in the slipstream.

'Can't you make this thing go faster?' shouted the Doctor.

'There is a seventy mile-an-hour speed limit,' said the Brigadier, averting his eyes from a speedometer now registering 90 mph.

'I knew we made a mistake not using Bessie,' shouted the Doctor. 'This thing's got no go in it.'

'I'm doing the best I can,' shouted the Brigadier, as he overtook a farm-cart and narrowly missed an oncoming motor-cyclist. 'It's no good if we get there dead.'

There was a long straight stretch of road ahead. The Brigadier kept his foot flat on the Jeep's floor. The speedometer climbed to 105 mph. 'That any better?' he called.

'I can't hear,' shouted the Doctor. 'You're going too fast.'

The long straight stretch ended in a twisting, narrow lane, and the Brigadier braked hard to avoid hitting a wall. With less windslip conversation was easier. 'I can't think what induced you to let Barker go to hospital,' said the Doctor.

'Look,' said the Brigadier, 'I only knew half of what had happened. It's all very easy for you, Doctor, because you've been involved in it all. For us on the outside, it takes some believing.

I'm still not convinced that that mark on Barker's arm isn't a rash of some sort.'

'Then why are you driving so fast?' asked the Doctor.

'Because,' said the Brigadier, 'there are times when I trust your judgement. Satisfied?'

'Yes,' said the Doctor. 'Fairly satisfied.'

The Brigadier gave the Doctor a sideways glance. Finally, he knew, you could always settle an argument by appealing to the Doctor's vanity. It was a little human-like quality that the Doctor had, and was one of the reasons why the Brigadier liked him.

'I think that must be it over there,' said the Doctor, pointing to a small building in what seemed to be its own grounds. 'Looks like a small hospital.'

The Brigadier raced the Jeep in the direction of the buildings. A private drive led off from the main road. At the side of the drive was a big sign reading: 'ST MARY'S COTTAGE HOSPITAL'. The Brigadier swung the Jeep into the drive. As they approached the main entrance of the hospital, swing doors suddenly flew open and Major Barker tumbled out on to the steps leading up to the entrance. A young doctor in a white coat and a nurse came through the doors after Major Barker, and the doctor tried to grab him. Major Barker got to his feet, knocked down the doctor, and stumbled down the steps. The nurse came after him.

'You must let us help you,' she called out.

The Brigadier stopped the Jeep and leapt to the ground to intercept Major Barker.

'Don't touch him,' the Doctor called. 'Let him go.'

Major Barker stood facing the Brigadier. Barker's face was now almost as red as the terrible mark on his arm. The young doctor had scrambled to his feet and came down the steps. 'I'll put you in a straitjacket if you carry on like that,' he called out.

'Major Barker,' said the Brigadier very calmly, 'you must go back into the hospital. You are ill. They want to help you.'

Barker swayed slightly, then put his hands to his throat and opened his mouth wide. 'I can't breathe,' he screamed, 'I'm being strangled.' He suddenly dropped in a heap on the gravel driveway as though all the strength had gone out of him. The young doctor and nurse were too startled to do anything. The Brigadier stepped forward and knelt by Major Barker.

'He's dead,' the Brigadier said, then straightened up.

'You can't be sure,' said the young doctor. 'Nurse, get the porters. We'll take him into Casualty immediately.'

'It's no good,' said the Brigadier. 'I may not be a doctor, but I know a dead man when I see one.'

'I still intend to feel for a pulse,' said the young doctor, and stepped forward to kneel by Major Barker.

'Keep back!' said the Brigadier.

The young doctor paused. 'Who are you people?'

The Doctor said, 'We came to warn you that that man is, or was, highly infectious.'

'I think that's something for me to decide,' said the young doctor. He took another step forward to inspect Major Barker.

'I told you to keep back!' The Brigadier drew his service revolver from its holster. The nurse and the young doctor looked at the gun in astonishment. 'Get back inside the hospital. If anyone leaves that building, I shall shoot to kill!' To underline his point, he thumbed back the gun's cock.

The young doctor and the nurse slowly went back up the steps to the swing-doors. There were other people in the hallway, looking through the glass panels of the doors. 'We shall telephone the police,' said the young doctor. 'We shall have you arrested!'

The Brigadier aimed his gun directly at the young doctor. 'Get back or I fire!'

The young doctor looked at the gun, then turned and fled through the swing-doors. The nurse followed.

'This place will have to be quarantined,' said the Doctor. He looked down at Barker's body. 'Poor man. But he's only the first.'

The Brigadier went back to the Jeep and picked up the R/T telephone. Within a moment he was speaking to Sergeant Hawkins at the research centre. 'Sergeant, have we got any sign yet of getting any reinforcements?'

The Sergeant's voice crackled over the 'phone. 'Not to my knowledge, sir, not unless Mr Masters promised you some.'

The Brigadier put his hand over the mouthpiece and turned to the Doctor. 'Any ideas, Doctor, how I get this place cordoned off with only six men, all of whom I need at the caves?'

'Possibly,' said the Doctor. 'Let me have the 'phone.' He took the instrument as he spoke. 'This is the Doctor speaking,

Sergeant Hawkins. Telephone the local Health Officer, whoever he is, and tell him that you are the registrar of St Mary's Cottage Hospital, and that you have got an outbreak of bubonic plague. If he doesn't know what you're talking about, mention that it killed seventy-five million people in the Middle Ages.'

The Sergeant asked, 'What if he asks me something technical, sir?'

'Give a sort of strangled sound over the 'phone,' said the Doctor, 'and pretend you've got the plague yourself. Then ring off.'

'Yes, sir,' said Hawkins.

'You see,' said the Doctor, handing back the 'phone to the Brigadier, 'that'll bring the whole of the Derbyshire police-force round here in no time. No one will be allowed in, and no one will be able to get out. Meantime, you hold the fort with that revolver.'

'And what are you going to do?' asked the Brigadier.

'Try to develop the antidote,' said the Doctor. 'Good luck.'

The Doctor jumped into the driver's seat of the Jeep, and drove away fast down the drive.

*

With Liz helping, the Doctor smeared some of the substance from the canister on to a rectangle of glass and put it under a microscope. At last the Doctor had managed to convince Dr Lawrence of the urgency of the situation, and the sick-bay laboratory had been made over to him to work in.

'What's it look like?' said Liz.

The Doctor adjusted the focus of the microscope. 'Nasty black blobs,' he said.

Dr Meredith hurried in. 'I've inoculated everyone in the Centre,' he said, 'but do you really think pumping antibiotics into people is any good against this stuff?'

'I've no idea,' said the Doctor. 'But it can't do any harm. Now what about my electron microscope?'

The Brigadier entered in time to hear the question. 'It'll be here in an hour, Doctor.'

The Doctor whirled round from the microscope. 'What's happened to that hospital?'

The Brigadier reported that the hospital had been entirely cordoned off by the Derbyshire police. 'And another thing,' he added, 'the Army is sending me reinforcements at last. Within half-an-hour I'll have every entrance to the caves guarded. How's the vaccine going?'

The Doctor gave the Brigadier a scathing look. 'I haven't even analysed the virus yet,' he said. 'All these new soldiers coming along here,' he went on, 'every one of them must be inoculated immediately they arrive.'

'I'll see to that,' said Dr Meredith.

'Another thing,' said the Doctor. 'We must have the least possible contact between all the people concerned. The Brigadier's reinforcements mustn't mix with anyone from the Centre, and even within the research centre people from different departments must have as little contact as possible.' He had a sudden thought. 'That man Masters – he was at the meeting with Major Barker! How's he travelling back to London?'

'He mentioned catching a train,' said Liz.

'Brigadier,' said the Doctor, 'you must stop that train right away.'

But the Brigadier had already scooped up a 'phone and was speaking into it. 'I don't mind if you have to put a tank across the railway line,' he was saying, 'that train must not reach London!'

*

The guard on the train to London came along the corridor of the first-class compartments to inspect tickets. The train had just lurched to a stop, which puzzled him. He looked out of the window, but it was now dark outside and he could only just see the backs of some cottages. Then the train started again, going very slowly. He slid open the door of a compartment where the blinds were down.

'Ticket, please, sir,' he said.

There was only one person in the compartment. He looked up and said: 'Pardon?'

The guard thought he knew the passenger's face. Surely he had seen the man on television, or his pictures in the newspaper. 'Your ticket, sir,' he repeated.

'Oh, yes.' The passenger fumbled for his ticket and produced it. His face was flushed, and he didn't seem at all well.

As the guard clipped the ticket he asked, 'Feeling all right, sir?'

'A bit tired,' said the man. 'Why is the train going so slowly?'

'No idea,' said the guard. Then he heard the familiar sound of the train's wheels bumping over points. He crossed to the compartment window, and looked out. 'They're putting us into a siding, sir,' he said, bewildered by this. The train again lurched to a stop.

The passenger also looked out of the window. 'Where are we?'

'Somewhere near Peterborough, I think,' said the guard.

'I must get to London immediately!' The passenger suddenly stood up and reached for his brief-case. 'Let me get by.'

'We're going to London,' said the guard.

'No, we're not,' said the passenger. 'You just said it yourself, they've put us into a siding. Let me get by.'

The passenger pushed by the guard to get to the corridor.

'You can't leave the train, sir,' called the guard. 'It's against the regulations. Only at recognised stations.'

But the passenger was already halfway down the corridor and was opening one of the doors. 'I have an important meeting to attend. I must get to London by some other means.'

The guard wanted to follow the passenger, to stop him from getting down on to the line. But somehow he felt terribly tired. He felt his forehead and decided he was running a temperature. It was strictly against regulations, but he turned and went back into the compartment and slumped down into one of the comfortable first-class seats. His ticket-clippers slipped from his fingers on to the floor. Then he blacked out.

*

Morka sat on what had been Okdel's special chair in the inner room. K'to entered.

'You summoned me,' said K'to.

'I have just inspected the caves,' said Morka. 'There are humans present, with weapons. Why are they not all dead?'

'Not all were killed instantly,' said K'to, 'even in our time.'

'Do not say "our time"!' thundered Morka. 'This *is* our time.'

'It is possible,' said K'to, with all the respect due to the new leader, 'that the virus may take longer with these new apes.'

'Or have they developed an antidote?'

'That is beyond their intelligence,' said K'to, more to please Morka than because he believed it himself. 'We need a human specimen in order to observe the effects of the virus. If necessary I might be able to develop a more virulent strain.'

'Then I shall return to the caves,' said Morka, 'and capture one of these humans with weapons.'

'There is another possibility,' said K'to. 'Could we not capture the creature that took the virus from Okdel?'

'How?'

'We know they have this special place,' said K'to, 'deep in the ground and close to our shelter. The shortest distance between

142

one place and another is a straight line.'

Morka was pleased with this idea. 'The rock melts easily,' he said. 'We made the tunnel to bring in air without difficulty.' He rose from the chair. 'We shall start now.'

*

Jock Tangye had never driven his hire-car to London before in all his years in business. He was just sitting down to a knife-and-fork tea with his wife when there was a banging on his front door. A man stood on his whitewashed doorstep, very well dressed but wild-eyed, and said, 'Do you run a taxi?'

'Yes,' said Jock, 'but I'm having my tea.'

'I'll give you ten pounds to drive me to London immediately,' said the man. 'Or twenty if you want.'

Jock didn't even bother to drink his cup of tea. Normally he drove villagers to go shopping in Peterborough, and charged them fifty pence each. Twenty pounds was his average weekly income.

'Don't I know your face?' he asked his passenger as they set off.

'Probably,' said the man, then seemed to doze off in the back seat.

Jock made his way to the A1 and headed south. Ninety minutes later he was hemmed in by fast-moving traffic going over the Brent Cross flyover. 'You'll have to tell me which way to go from here,' he called over his shoulder. 'I don't know London.' There was no answer from the back seat. He looked at the man through his rear mirror. The passenger's face was deathly white, his mouth hung open. Jock pulled into the side, stopped, turned towards his passenger. 'Are you all right?' The passenger didn't move.

Jock scrambled out of his car, stood in the road and tried to wave down some oncoming cars. Headlights flashed at him and hooters were sounded in anger. The cars swept by him. He cried out to them, 'Stop! Someone help me!' But none of the cars stopped. He was almost in tears, sweat dripping from his forehead. Then he saw a panda-car approaching with the word 'POLICE' in illuminated letters. He stood right in front of it to force it to stop. A young police-officer looked out from the driver's window.

'What's the matter?' The young policeman sounded angry. People in London didn't expect to be stopped, or even to have to speak to someone they didn't know.

'My passenger,' said Jock, 'have a look at him.'

The panda-car pulled into the side, and the young policeman got out. 'You got someone drunk in there?' He produced a torch, and leaned into the back of Jock's car. 'Now then, wakey-wakey,' he shouted. Then he went very quiet and turned to Jock. 'You know who this is?'

'No idea,' said Jock.

'Right Honourable Frederick Masters,' said the young policeman. 'And he's dead.' The policeman crossed back to his panda-car and took up the radio-telephone. Jock watched on, bewildered by all the noise and the traffic. Then, suddenly, he felt very ill.

*

Sergeant Hawkins put down the 'phone in the conference room, crossed to a map of Britain pinned on the wall. He selected two pin-flags from a box under the map, stuck them in London. There were already three flags stuck in Derbyshire, one near Peterborough. The Brigadier entered, saw Hawkins putting in the new flags.

'So it's got to London?' said the Brigadier.

'Mr Masters,' said Hawkins, 'and a man with a hire-car. There's also a young policeman very ill in the Royal Free Hospital.'

'What's the one in Peterborough?' said the Brigadier.

'The guard on the train. He died an hour ago in hospital there.'

'We'll have to put the whole country in quarantine,' said the Brigadier. 'At least we can stop the rest of the world being affected.'

The 'phone rang, and Hawkins answered it. 'Research Centre, Wenley Moor,' he said, 'Sergeant Hawkins speaking.' He listened, then frowned. 'Right, thanks.' He put down the 'phone. 'It looks like we're too late, sir. Orly Airport, Paris – two of them gone down with it, from a flight from London.'

'That's impossible,' said the Brigadier. 'What's the connection?'

'Both nurses,' said Sergeant Hawkins, 'from the Royal Free Hospital, London, going away for the weekend.'

Without a word the Brigadier turned on his heel and left the conference room. Sergeant Hawkins unrolled a map of the world. He carefully attached sticky tape to the two top corners, then stuck the map on the wall. Then he selected two pin-flags and stuck them in Paris.

*

In the laboratory the Doctor was supervising the installation of an electron microscope. The Brigadier entered.

'Doctor,' said the Brigadier, 'this thing is spreading like wildfire. There's two dead in London, now two in Paris.'

'Can't all international flights be stopped?' asked Liz.

'I rather think it's too late,' said the Brigadier. 'Have you made any progress, Doctor?'

'It's a bit like a journey in the dark,' said the Doctor. 'I won't know that I've arrived until I'm there.'

The Brigadier sat down on one of the few available chairs. He touched his forehead, then looked at the glistening sweat on his fingers. 'Perhaps we'd better all have some more antibiotics,' he said.

Liz gave a quick look at the Doctor, and the Doctor nodded. 'Get young Meredith to serve up antibiotics all round,' he said. 'And tell him to be quick about it.'

*

Morka, K'to, and three other reptile men stood and looked at a section of the metal wall of their shelter.

'We should start here,' said K'to.

'How can you be sure?' asked Morka.

'I have listened to the wall with one of our sound-detecting devices,' said K'to. 'One can hear the humans' voices at this point. Here, we are closest to their scientific place beneath the ground.'

'Then we commence,' said Morka.

Morka looked hard at the metal wall. Then his third eye began to pulsate, glowing red. K'to's third eye followed, and then the third eyes of the other reptile men. The metal in front of them glowed red hot and then white hot, and soon it fell away in molten flakes. Behind was the solid rock of the caves. That, too, began to melt before the heat-force of the reptile men.

*

Liz, Dr Meredith, and the Brigadier watched on intently as the Doctor poured liquids into a phial. By now every chemical in the laboratory was standing in a jungle of bottles and phials on the working-top by the electron microscope. The Doctor put the phial into an agitator, and pressed a button. The phial whirled round, mixing the liquid chemicals. Then he stopped the agitator, and drew off some drops of the liquid on to a glass and put the glass under the electron microscope.

'How are you feeling?' Liz asked the Brigadier.

'Not too bad,' he said, although she could see he was perspiring freely.

'If the virus strain knows what it's about,' said Dr Meredith, 'it'll soon find a way to overcome the antibiotics.'

'What'll happen then?' asked the Brigadier.

'That will be fatal,' said Dr Meredith, as though quoting from a medical textbook.

'Thank you very much,' said the Brigadier. 'That's most comforting.' He spoke up to the Doctor. 'It seems I'm going to be dead soon, Doctor. Any chance you can hurry things along?'

'Give him some more antibiotics,' said the Doctor, not looking up from the microscope.

'We haven't got any more,' said Dr Meredith. 'We've run out.'

'Charming,' said the Brigadier. 'That makes my day.'

The Doctor held himself very still. 'I think this is it,' he said quietly.

Dr Meredith crossed to the microscope. 'May I see?'

'Later,' said the Doctor. 'It's only a few blobs squirming about. But *my* blobs are definitely killing off *their* blobs!' He turned to the Brigadier. 'Where's our guinea pig?'

'In a bed, in a ward, in a coma,' said the Brigadier. 'I brought in the ambulance driver who took Major Barker to hospital.'

'Excellent.' The Doctor plunged a syringe into the phial he had just mixed. 'Now let's get this into him and see what happens.'

The Doctor held the syringe point upwards and marched out of the laboratory.

'Doesn't he ever get tired?' asked Dr Meredith.

'No,' said the Brigadier. 'He just gets impossible to work with sometimes, that's all.'

*

Morka stood now in a tunnel of perfectly smooth rock, just wide enough for his shoulders. He faced the rock before him, concentrating on to it the power of his third eye. The rock glowed white with heat and melted. The concentration took all his energy, but he continued until he knew it was impossible to go on any longer. He stopped concentrating, and walked back through the narrow tunnel to where the other reptile men were waiting. Immediately another reptile man stepped forward to take Morka's place, while Morka regained his strength of concentration.

'Many of the humans must be dead by now,' said K'to, to please Morka. He could see how tired Morka was. Morka took longer spells at melting the rock than any of the others.

'We should have activated the other shelters,' said Morka. 'It is wrong that we alone should have to fight this vermin.' He stood thinking, watching the back of the reptile man now taking a turn at melting the rock. 'What if they do find an antidote? Can your science save us then?'

'There is something else,' said K'to, 'something I have set my assistants to work on. But let us first capture this creature that pretends it understands science. Then we shall see.'

*

The Doctor, Liz, and the Brigadier stood round the sick-bay bed while Dr Meredith felt the ambulance driver's pulse. 'It's normal,' he said, excitement in his voice, 'it's definitely normal.'

'Let me see,' said the Doctor, and pushed Dr Meredith out of the way to hold the sick man's wrist.

The Brigadier whispered to Liz, 'Such charming manners he has.' Liz told the Brigadier to shut up.

'Yes,' said the Doctor, 'I think you're right.'

'Thank you,' said Dr Meredith, the excitement replaced with a touch of ice in his voice. 'I may not understand lizards and reptiles, but I can tell when a pulse is normal.'

The Doctor stepped back. 'My dear fellow, I'm terribly sorry. How very rude of me.'

The Brigadier spoke up. 'When you two have finished exchanging pleasantries, would you mind saying what we do now? You've saved one man. There are people dropping dead all over the world by now!'

'It's obvious,' said the Doctor, 'we've got to 'phone the formula to London so that they can get the antidote into mass production right away. You get London on the 'phone, Brigadier. I'll get the formula.' He moved to the door, then stopped and turned to Dr Meredith. 'Oh, and you…'

'Yes?' said Dr Meredith.

The Doctor indicated the man in the bed. 'Give the poor fellow a cup of tea or something.' Then the Doctor was gone.

'I'll start that call to London,' said the Brigadier, and followed the Doctor out.

Liz went closer to the man in the bed. 'You're sure he's getting better?'

'Every test proves normal,' said Dr Meredith. 'But he's exhausted. His body's been fighting this thing, and it's knocked him out. That's just normal sleep. Now I think we should leave him alone.'

Liz left the sick-bay and went down the corridor to the conference room. The maps on the walls were now peppered with pin-flags. There were many flags in the Midlands, but the greatest concentration was in the London area. In the map of the world flags had been pinned into Paris, Frankfurt, and now Sergeant Hawkins was just pinning one into Belgrade. The Brigadier was on the outside 'phone.

'Yes sir,' said the Brigadier, 'we've got the answer to it. I'm going to read the formula to you now, and then it must be produced in quantity immediately and shipped all over Europe.' He looked up at Liz and snapped his fingers. 'The formula, please.'

She said, 'I thought the Doctor was getting it. He had it

written down in the laboratory.'

The Brigadier cupped the 'phone. 'Well, please will you get it from him immediately! I've got the Ministry on the 'phone now.'

Liz hurried out and ran all the way to the laboratory. As she approached the laboratory she noticed the strange smell of burning in the air. She opened the door and stood there too terrified to speak. Two reptile men were dragging the unconscious Doctor towards a hole that had been bored in the wall. Without noticing Liz they disappeared down what appeared to be a smooth-walled passageway. The hole closed in, as though it had never been there. Then Liz started to scream.

The Brigadier was the first to get there. 'What the devil's

going on?'

Liz fell into the Brigadier's arms, her body quivering. 'They've got him. Took him prisoner. He may be dead. Through that wall!'

Dr Meredith had also heard the screams and came running along the corridor. The Brigadier pushed Liz towards him. 'She's got hysterics,' he said. Dr Meredith took Liz in his arms. The Brigadier crossed to the wall, felt it with the palm of his hand. 'It's still warm,' he said. He turned to Liz. 'Well, we've still got to give London that formula.'

'But the Doctor,' she cried, 'they've taken him prisoner!'

'Miss Shaw,' said the Brigadier, 'we are concerned about saving the lives of millions of people.' He looked at the work top; it was littered with pieces of paper on which the Doctor had noted down the many formulae he had tried. 'Which of these is the right formula?'

Liz crossed to the work top, looked at the Doctor's notes. 'I don't know,' she said.

The Brigadier turned to Dr Meredith. 'Have you any idea which is the right one?'

Dr Meredith shook his head. 'I wasn't in here all the time while the Doctor was working.'

'Well, we can't just stand here doing nothing,' the Brigadier said, and Liz noted a touch of hysteria in his voice now. 'One of these bits of paper may save the entire human race!'

Liz looked again at the Doctor's scribble now. She tried very hard to remember which was the last one he had made. 'It might be this one,' she said, choosing the one she thought she had seen him write last.

'All right,' said the Brigadier. 'Then let's 'phone it through to London.'

'Just one moment,' said Dr Meredith. 'What if Miss Shaw has made a mistake?'

'In that eventuality,' said the Brigadier, 'we shall all be dead fairly soon. Satisfied?' He took Liz's arm and marched her down the corridor back to the conference room and the telephone.

18

A Hot World

The Doctor came to in one of the prisoner cages. K'to and Morka looked through the bars at him. 'How many humans have died in the epidemic?' K'to asked.

'Only a few,' said the Doctor. 'The majority will survive.'

'Speak the truth,' said Morka, and his third eye glowed red for a fraction of a second. The Doctor felt sudden pain through his arms and legs while the third eye glowed. 'What you say is impossible!'

K'to was more reasonable. 'You have discovered a cure?'

'Yes,' said the Doctor. 'Soon all the humans will be immune to your virus. Your plan has failed, just as your leader wanted it to fail.'

'That old leader is dead,' said Morka. 'I am now the leader.'

Another reptile man came up to Morka. 'The plan is now in operation. A large battle rages in the caves.' Morka acknowledged the report, and the reptile man went away.

'It's useless having battles in the caves,' said the Doctor. 'You should be making peace, not war. Even if you defeat the soldiers now in the caves, they will send more and more against you. You are totally outnumbered.'

'The battle is part of our plan,' said Morka. 'It doesn't matter if we lose this battle in the caves. While you slept in your cage, *our* soldiers attacked yours. All soldiers will be withdrawn from your research centre and put into the caves to fight us.'

'While you go back into the research centre,' asked the Doctor, 'through that tunnel you made?'

'Of course.' Morka turned to K'to. 'Is the destructor ready?'

'We need only the power,' said K'to. 'The electricity created by the humans.'

'Then you are going to be unlucky,' the Doctor said, 'because the nuclear generator has been shut down, thanks to you.'

'You will reactivate it for us,' said Morka. 'Either that or die.'

'The alternative doesn't sound very attractive,' said the Doctor. 'What does this destructor do?'

'A destructor,' said Morka, 'is something with which you destruct something else.' The scales of his cheeks quivered, which the Doctor took for laughter.

'Don't imagine you can destroy the human race with some gadget,' said the Doctor. 'It's too great a task even for your science!'

'We shall not try again to destroy the humans,' said K'to. 'Instead we shall change the world as they know it.' He turned to Morka. 'We should leave now.'

Morka looked at the lock on the cage door; his third eye glowed, and the lock clicked open. 'Come out of your cage,' he said. 'If you displease us, you will die instantly.'

The Doctor came out from the cage. 'You keep harping on my imminent death,' he said. 'Can't we talk about something else?'

'He jokes,' said K'to. 'The little furry animals were always chattering and joking amongst themselves. You see, they have not really changed.'

'Follow me,' said Morka, and walked towards a section of wall which had let into it a perfectly smooth-walled passage. At the opening to the passage, Morka stopped. 'You will go first.' He gave a signal, and a number of other reptile men came forward. 'We shall all follow you.'

The Doctor walked down the narrow passage. 'Is there an opening at the other end?' he asked.

'There will be,' said Morka, right behind the Doctor. 'Continue.'

The Doctor continued until the passageway came to an abrupt stop. He felt Morka come up close behind him. Morka was directing his third eye over the Doctor's shoulder. In a moment the wall of rock in front of the Doctor vanished and he found himself looking into the laboratory in the research centre. 'Walk forward slowly,' said Morka. 'The other humans must see you first.'

The Doctor slowly crossed the floor of the laboratory. He took a quick glance at his notes on the work top. The correct formula was missing, so someone had had the sense to know which it was. 'Where to?' he asked without looking back.

'Continue until we find humans,' Morka said.

The Doctor paused. 'If you kill anyone I shall not help you.'

'Forward,' said Morka. 'We may allow those down here to live a little longer when all those on the surface are dead. It depends if they are useful.'

'Practical thinking,' said the Doctor. He stepped out into the corridor. Further down the corridor the Brigadier and Liz were standing at the lift door. The Brigadier was pressing the lift button. As though by instinct the Brigadier turned round.

'Doctor!' he exclaimed. 'We thought you'd been taken prisoner. Your antidote's working fine, but now all hell's let loose in the caves. Reptiles everywhere. I've sent all my men into the caves, and now the 'phone's dead and the lift won't work…' The Brigadier's voice trailed off as he saw Morka and other reptile men come up behind the Doctor.

'Don't make any hasty moves, Brigadier,' the Doctor said.

'We are all prisoners now. I'm sorry.'

'Guard those apes,' said Morka, and two reptile men hurried up to the Brigadier and Liz. He turned to the Doctor. 'Take us to the source of your power.'

The Doctor walked slowly towards the cyclotron room. The Brigadier and Liz were pushed alongside the Doctor. The three were kept bunched together, so that all could be killed instantly if they made a wrong move. As the trio entered the cyclotron room Dr Lawrence and the technicians looked up first in surprise then in horror as the reptile men crowded in.

'The nuclear generator must be reactivated,' said the Doctor to Dr Lawrence. 'They need your power.'

Dr Lawrence's face was crimson with anger, the first time the Doctor had seen him show any real emotion. 'No! You creatures have tried to ruin the work of this research centre. You have probably ruined my career…' His protest was cut short as Morka's third eye glowed a vicious scarlet. Dr Lawrence fell dead to the floor.

'All apes look at the body,' said Morka. 'It is an example of what will happen to you if you are not obedient to your masters.' He looked slowly round the group of technicians, satisfied that they were all sufficiently terrified.

The Doctor heard a trundling sound, looked behind himself and saw reptile men dragging in a tubular object on four tiny wheels. 'The destructor?' he asked.

K'to answered. 'You will now connect the destructor to your nuclear generator.'

'I must know the purpose of this machine,' the Doctor said. 'Otherwise I cannot properly help you.'

K'to looked to Morka, as though asking if he may explain the purpose of the destructor to the Doctor. Morka made no sign that the Doctor could understand; his reply to K'to must have been by some kind of telepathy – thought-waves between the two reptile men. K'to turned back to the Doctor. 'Since we entered our shelter,' he explained, 'and went into total sleep, the temperature of this planet, *our* planet, has changed. We have detected some invisible barrier between the rays of the sun and the surface of Earth. Microwaves from the destructor will disperse this barrier, removing it for ever.'

'The van Allen belt is indestructible,' said the Doctor, hopefully. He could not be sure this was true.

The Brigadier asked: 'Do you mind telling me what you two are talking about?'

'The van Allen belt,' said the Doctor, 'is named after the scientist who discovered its existence. It envelops the Earth, and protects us from the sun's most harmful rays. Without it people would die of sunburn on a cloudy day.'

'Your people will die,' said Morka. 'We reptiles survive best in heat. All of you apes here, under the ground, will live as long as we find you useful. All mammals on the surface will die.'

'Now look here, Doctor,' said the Brigadier, 'you mustn't do anything to help these…' He almost said 'creatures', but thought better of it. 'These people,' he said.

'We have no alternative,' said the Doctor. He turned to Liz. 'Miss Shaw, I'm going to need your assistance.' Then he looked to the waiting technicians. 'Miss Shaw and I can manage to stoke up the nuclear generator between us. I suggest you all go to your usual controls and keep well back from the generator.' The Doctor crossed to the nuclear generator control console, followed by Liz. 'I take it you can understand these controls,' he said to her, 'they're quite simple. I want you to feed in the uranium rods one at a time as I tell you.'

The Brigadier broke away from the reptile man who was guarding him. 'Doctor, do you know what you're doing? I understand this apparatus is all highly dangerous!'

'Even a tin-opener,' said the Doctor, 'can be dangerous if

not properly used. All this apparatus does is to make heat, great heat, when the uranium rods are lowered into place. If you're worried, you can watch them being lowered in through this panel.' The Doctor indicated the panel of thick plate glass; beyond, one could see the uranium rods suspended over the holes into which they were to be dropped. 'The heat makes steam for the turbine, and the turbine makes the electricity that our friends need for their destructor. It's all very elementary.'

Morka stepped in between the Doctor and the Brigadier. 'If this creature bothers you,' he said, indicating the Brigadier, 'I can kill him for you.'

'That's very kind of you,' the Doctor said, 'but that won't be necessary. He is quite a useful ape sometimes. Liz, are you ready?'

Liz nodded.

K'to said, 'You must first connect our destructor to your power supply.'

'I thought you would use induction,' said the Doctor. 'That is how you stole electricity before.'

'He jokes,' said Morka. 'Explain.'

'With induction,' said K'to, taking the Doctor quite seriously, 'we lost a great deal of your power. Induction is not as efficient as direct contact.'

The Doctor looked round the technicians. 'Can one of you connect this thing to the main power supply, please?' None of the technicians moved, either through fear or not wishing to help the reptile invaders. 'Come along now,' said the Doctor, 'just one volunteer, please.'

Miss Travis, the young technician who had brought in coffee for Mr Masters that the Doctor had drunk, stepped forward. 'Perhaps I can do it.'

K'to immediately stepped up to Miss Travis with the end of the cable that led from the destructor. 'You make connection,' he said.

Miss Travis looked at the cable. 'I'll need a knife,' she said. No one responded.

'Surely someone has a knife,' the Doctor said. 'We can't stop the greatest scientific experiment in Earth's history through not having a knife between us!'

Still no one responded.

Liz said, 'I believe the Brigadier has a penknife.'

'If that's the case,' said the Doctor, 'kindly produce it immediately.'

Slowly, without a word, the Brigadier drew from his pocket a boy's penknife and handed it to Miss Travis. 'Thank you,' she said, and set to work cutting away the coating of the destructor's cable to the bare wires inside.

The Doctor turned to Liz. 'Lower in number one rod now, please.'

Liz moved one of the reactor controls. The Brigadier squinted through the smoked panel of glass and saw one of the hanging uranium rods slowly sink down into the hole beneath it. Instantly there was a hum of power in the room, and the fingers of a dozen control dials quivered. The Doctor, however, seemed to be occupied with the mass of wires and fuses immediately under the reactor controls.

'Number one rod in position,' Liz reported.

'Excellent,' said the Doctor, not looking up, 'now lower in number two.'

Liz moved another control. The second uranium rod slowly sank into the hole beneath it. The fingers of the dials quivered again, registering greater power output. K'to looked down at the Doctor curiously.

'What are you doing?' asked K'to.

The Doctor briefly looked up from his work on the wires under the control panel. 'This plant clearly has to produce more

159

power than it has ever done before. I'm trying to make sure that that is possible.'

K'to didn't seem satisfied. 'Power is not increased by interference with the circuits of the controls,' he said.

'I am trying to adapt the controls,' said the Doctor. 'Look, do you really want to stop this whole delicate operation for me to explain in detail how I am trying to help you?'

Morka stepped in between K'to and the Doctor. 'The ape is showing obedience.' He looked down at the Doctor. 'More power, immediately!'

'Certainly,' said the Doctor. 'Liz, lower in number three rod now.'

Liz moved the third control in the row on the console. The hum of power was now ear-splitting and the control dials were nearing the word 'DANGER'. One of the technicians stood up to protest. 'You're making more power than an atomic bomb, Doctor! You'll kill us all...'

Morka swung round to the technician, his third eye ablaze with redness. The technician gasped, then fell across his desk. Morka looked at the other humans. 'No more talk!' Then he turned back to the Doctor. 'More power, immediately!'

The Doctor said, 'Liz, lower in number four rod.'

Liz moved the 'four' control.

'Now five and six together,' the Doctor said, straightening up from his work on the circuits under the console.

Liz moved the final two controls. The fifth and sixth uranium rods slowly sank into their respective holes. The fingers of all the dials held steady at a point well beyond the word 'DANGER'.

Miss Travis had finished her work exposing the wires of the destructor unit's cable. 'I'm ready to connect,' she told the Doctor.

'Thank you,' said the Doctor. 'I shall take over now.' He took the destructor's cable, crossed to a wall terminal point, checked that it was turned to 'Off', then connected the two bared wires of the cable. Then he pulled a switch beside the terminal point to its 'On' position. He crossed back to the control console, put his hand on the lever that would make the final connection of power between the generator and the wall terminal point. 'Let us see how well your destructor works,' he said.

As the Doctor started to move the lever, K'to sprang forward hissing. 'It's a trick! I know it is a trick!'

But the Doctor had already pulled the lever. The destructor hummed with power for a few seconds; then a huge crack appeared along one side of it and smoke belched from the crack.

K'to turned to Morka. 'Kill him! He has destroyed the destructor!'

Morka turned to the Doctor, but his third eye did not yet glow its fatal red colour. 'Stop everything! Turn off the generator!'

'I can't,' said the Doctor. 'I've destroyed the circuits of the control console. The reactor is at this moment turning into an atomic bomb. In a few moments it will explode. You will die with us. The radiation will leak into your own shelter, destroying all those of you not killed instantly by the explosion. I can only advise you to get back to your shelter as quickly as possible and seal yourselves up. Then you may be safe.'

Morka asked K'to, 'Can this be true?'

K'to didn't answer. He was staring at the destructor as it slowly melted with heat. A watery tear ran down the scales of his cheek. 'With the destructor we could have returned our planet to what it was when we were the masters.'

Morka's third eye flashed red at K'to, and K'to winced in pain. 'Can this be true?' he repeated.

'It is all true,' said K'to. 'We must return to our shelter or

161

die.' He looked again at the destructor. It was now a mound of shapeless metal on the floor.

Morka looked round the room at the humans. 'I do not understand,' he said. 'You have sacrificed yourselves so that other apes may live. My people would not have behaved like that.'

'Perhaps,' said the Doctor, 'that is why the apes – the humans – are such a successful species. They do not only think of themselves.'

'Well, apes,' said Morka, 'you can all die together in the explosion.' He signalled to K'to and the other reptile men, turned and led them away. None of the humans moved a muscle until the last of the reptile men had gone. Then the Brigadier broke into a grin.

'Jolly good work, Doctor,' he said. 'Now for goodness' sake turn this thing off.'

'What I said was true,' the Doctor answered. 'I can't turn it off.'

The Brigadier looked stunned. 'Are you aware that the lift isn't working? We're all trapped down here!'

The Doctor turned to the technicians. 'If any of you has any idea how to stop the generator from becoming an atomic bomb, now would be a good time to speak up.'

'I think I know how,' said Miss Travis. 'The control console has a fail-safe mechanism. May I show you?' She crossed to the console, looked under the panel where the Doctor had dislocated the control circuit. 'It's here,' she said. 'All we have to do is to pull out a fuse.'

Miss Travis calmly put her hand in among the now tangled wires of the control circuits, reached as far as possible and pulled out a single fuse. Instantly all the uranium rods started to rise up into their neutral positions. The fingers of the dials slowly sank from 'DANGER' back to 'ZERO'.

162

'Miss Travis,' said the Brigadier, 'you are a very level-headed young woman. I'm sure you will become a great scientist one day.'

'I don't know about that,' she said. 'After all this, I think I'd rather work in a bank.'

19

The Lie

The Doctor and Liz got into Bessie in the research centre car park. The Brigadier had come to say goodbye.

'Going straight back to London?' asked the Brigadier.

'Yes,' said the Doctor.

'No,' said Liz.

'Well, make your minds up,' the Brigadier said.

'Since we're in Derbyshire,' Liz said, 'I want to see over some of the potteries. You know, Denby and Crown Derby.'

'What a good idea,' the Brigadier said. 'I wish I could join you.'

'How long are you staying on here?' asked the Doctor.

The Brigadier shrugged. 'Just one or two things to clear up,' he said. 'Routine matters.'

'You do understand the caves must not be touched,' the Doctor said. 'I want to return here next week with a team of scientists to try to make peaceful contact with the reptile men. There's a living museum down there, and if we can get on friendly terms with them there's a great deal we can learn about the origin of life on this planet.'

'On my honour,' the Brigadier said. 'If I so much as see a reptile man, I shall go out of my way to be nice to him.'

'You don't really take this seriously,' the Doctor said. 'These creatures have as much right to this planet as you have. I'm going to ask the Prime Minister to have it put to the United

Nations that the reptile people be formally invited to share the world.'

'Don't worry,' the Brigadier said. He looked at his watch, and seemed now to want to get rid of the Doctor and Liz. 'No harm will come to your reptiles. Now you'd better be off. Enjoy your trip to the potteries!'

'Possibly,' said the Doctor. He started the engine. 'Where are all your soldiers?'

'My soldiers?' said the Brigadier, as though he might be trying to hide something. 'Oh, they're out and about, cleaning up the mess and all that.' He again glanced at his watch.

'I see,' said the Doctor, realising that there was something the Brigadier didn't want him to know. 'Well, no more violence or killing. I'll see you in London.'

The Doctor slowly drove Bessie out of the car park and down the gravel road to the main road. As they turned into the main road he said, 'The Brigadier's got something up his sleeve, you know.'

Liz didn't answer. She just looked straight ahead down the road.

The Doctor slowed down the car and stopped; 'Something's going on that I don't know about,' he said. 'And you know what it is!'

Liz turned to him. 'Doctor, not everyone thinks like you…'

Her words were interrupted by a series of violent explosions. The Doctor turned and looked towards the main opening to the caves. A huge cloud of smoke and dust was belching out of the cave. Then there was another explosion, and the entrance to the cave collapsed in a huge deluge of huge rocks.

'He's sealed them in,' the Doctor said quietly.

Liz nodded. 'He had to. They'd never have accepted sharing this world.'

The Doctor felt anger rising in him. 'We've lost the chance

to find out now,' he said. 'We shall never know.'

The Doctor started up the car again and continued along the main road in silence.

About the Author

Born in 1924, Malcolm Hulke was a prolific and respected television writer from the 1950s until the 1970s, and wrote the definitive script-writing guide: *Writing for Television*. His writing credits included the early science fiction *Pathfinders* series, as well as *The Avengers*.

Malcolm Hulke was first approached to write for *Doctor Who* when the series was beginning production in 1963, but his idea for 'The Hidden Planet' was not pursued. In 1967, he wrote 'The Faceless Ones' (with David Ellis) for the Second Doctor. By 1969, Hulke's friend and occasional writing partner Terrance Dicks was Script Editor for *Doctor Who* and needed a ten-part story to replace other scripts and write out Patrick Troughton's Doctor. Together, they wrote 'The War Games', which for the first time explained the Doctor's origins and introduced his people, the Time Lords.

Hulke continued to write for *Doctor Who*, providing a story for each of the Third Doctor's five seasons. His scripts were notable for including adversaries that were not villainous simply for the sake of it, but who had a valid point of view and grievance. 'The Silurians' – which he novelised as 'The Cave Monsters' – is a good example of this, and the reptile men, like their aquatic 'cousins' the Sea Devils, are well remembered.

Malcolm Hulke died in 1979, soon after completing his novelisation of 'The War Games', which was published a few months after his death.

DOCTOR WHO AND THE CAVE MONSTERS
Between the Lines

Universal-Tandem's Target imprint began its *Doctor Who* range with reprints of three stories from the 1960s. The new series of novelisations then got properly under way with *Doctor Who and the Auton Invasion* by Terrance Dicks and *Doctor Who and the Cave Monsters* by Malcolm Hulke, both published in paperback on Thursday 17 January 1974. The covers and internal illustrations (used in this edition) were by Chris Achilleos.

This new edition re-presents that 1974 publication. While a few minor errors or inconsistencies have been corrected, no attempt has been made to update or modernise the text – this is *Doctor Who and the Cave Monsters* as originally written and published. This means that the novel retains certain stylistic and editorial practices that were current in 1973 (when the book was written and prepared for publication) but which have since adapted or changed. Most obviously, measurements are given in the then-standard imperial system of weights and measures: a yard is equivalent to 0.9144 metres; three feet make a yard, and a foot is 30 centimetres; twelve inches make a foot, and an inch is 25.4 millimetres.

Terrance Dicks's adaptation of Robert Holmes's 'Spearhead from Space' embellishes and resequences the television episodes quite extensively, especially when it comes to giving the serial's many minor characters a variety of back-stories and letting the reader in on their thoughts. Adapting his own scripts for 'The Silurians', Malcolm Hulke goes even further.

Rather than attempt to pack all seven episodes (almost three hours of television) into a 45,000-word novel, Hulke opts to rewrite his story from scratch, even rewording the majority of the dialogue. He dispenses entirely with the serial's opening scene, in which the technicians Spencer and Davis are attacked by a dinosaur while potholing. The event is instead recounted later by other characters, as is the Doctor's first encounter with Dr Quinn. On TV, this scene shows Quinn being politely evasive and culminates with the Doctor's discovery that the power-loss log has several pages missing. A number of scenes showing the research centre at work – and suffering power losses – are combined into one for the novelisation, in the process losing a moment in which the Doctor helps to stabilise the cyclotron. Also gone is the Doctor's night-long examination (equipped only with his sonic screwdriver, to Dr Lawrence's disgust) of the cyclotron.

A soldier's report in Chapter 8 replaces a screened visit by the Doctor and the Brigadier to see Doris Squire in hospital. The tell-tale presence of Bessie at the cave entrance alerts the Brigadier to the Doctor's expedition in Chapter 15, rather than Liz Shaw admitting to Masters that she knows where the Doctor's gone. In print, the Brigadier takes a far smaller force into the caves in Chapter 15 than he does on TV, and his grim return, having 'lost a lot of men', is dropped completely. Episode 6 features an extensive sequence of montages and scenes showing the Doctor experimenting to find a cure for the virus while Liz and the Brigadier take reports of the epidemic's spread and fend off demands for a formula. This is all heavily compressed here, with an electron microscope facilitating a much more rapid discovery of the necessary drug. On television, the cure comes too late for Dr Lawrence, who is an early victim of the plague. And the Doctor has one last confrontation with a Silurian after the reactor has been closed

170

down, which culminates with the Brigadier shooting the creature dead – again absent here.

Yet Hulke's novelisation does much more than simply compress his original storyline. Many scenes are revised or replaced. Miss Dawson is present at Quinn's death, which is later discovered by Dr Meredith not the Doctor. This also removes Miss Dawson's important intervention in Episode 4, revealing that Quinn has been killed by a Silurian and so apparently confirming that the creatures are hostile. The effects on the staff of working in the cyclotron room, including Liz Shaw's headache, are all but absent from the book. When the technician Roberts breaks down on television, he is merely restrained; here, Hulke has him inadvertently killed by Major Barker. The later threat of a police investigation into this helps tip the Major over the edge, a plot development not seen on TV. And the concluding chapter plays up the Brigadier's keenness to see the Doctor depart, but downplays the Doctor's disappointed dismay when the reptile base is blown up.

The main supporting characters are all given greatly expanded backgrounds and new motivations: Matthew Quinn, the son of a famous physicist, whose on-screen eagerness to make his mark is given an extra streak of ruthlessness; Charles Lawrence, now a markedly less unsympathetic character, but whose desperation to preserve his professional reputation remains; Phyllis Dawson, an unwilling spinster, who follows years of manipulation by her mother with misplaced loyalty to Quinn, even when he begins to blackmail her. Hulke relates Dr Quinn and Miss Dawson's walks across the moors and shared lunches, and allows Dr Lawrence to reminisce over his excitement on being appointed director at Wenley Moor and his prep school days with 'Freddie' Masters. Masters himself is now a Member of Parliament, introducing a small error – Permanent Under-Secretary is a Civil Service not Government role.

Several lesser characters, too, are fleshed out or invented for the novel. One scene in the fourth episode features a slightly supercilious research centre scientist called Travis; here, Travis becomes Miss Travis, initially a coffee-maker, but eventually key to preventing a reactor explosion. A taxi driver, given a handful of barely audible lines in Episode 7, becomes Jock Tangye, abandoning his tea for a week's wages and promptly succumbing to the epidemic. As well as gaining various privates and corporals, UNIT loses an officer, as the TV story's Captain Hawkins and Sergeant Hart are combined into the book's Sergeant Hawkins. In the serial, the unfortunate – and rather unfit – Sergeant Hart fails to prevent the absconding of the research centre's wounded security officer.

The portrait of Major Barker is also greatly extended from that of Major Baker, his television counterpart. Baker is presented as obsessively conscientious, understandably convinced that the 'monsters' are nothing more than saboteurs, and becoming increasingly unhinged as the story progresses. A line in Episode 1 explains that Baker 'slipped up badly once some years ago. He's been trying to make up for it ever since.' Hulke's novel goes into the detail of that past slip-up, recounting his experiences combating the IRA, the republican paramilitary group that conducted a terrorist campaign in Northern Ireland and mainland Britain from 1969. Hulke also makes Barker's psychotic patriotism and xenophobia key to several points in the worsening situation. This is a theme the writer explored in other *Doctor Who* stories, including 'The Ambassadors of Death', which Hulke helped to rewrite from David Whitaker's original scripts.

The series regulars are also presented rather differently to their TV equivalents. The Brigadier is to some extent an amalgamation of the strait-laced military officer of 1970 and the slightly softer, more parodic figure he gradually became: his 'That'll show 'em' exclamation about 'foreign competitors' in Chapter 2 could have slipped unnoticed into one of Lethbridge-Stewart's later TV stories like 'Planet of the Spiders' or 'Robot'.

The characterisation of Liz Shaw, meanwhile, gives no hint of the highly qualified scientist who assists the Third Doctor throughout his first season of television adventures. There is no mention of her degrees in physics, medicine and a dozen other subjects, and the only clue that she might be more than decorative comes in Chapter 8, when she is left at Squire's farm to conduct a forensic check. Where 'The Silurians' shows the Doctor and Liz working together to find a cure for the plague, *Doctor Who and the Cave Monsters* leaves the science to the Doctor – to the extent that Liz simply tries to remember which formula the Doctor had written last. If anything, Hulke's depiction of Liz here owes more to her successor as the Doctor's companion, Jo Grant, though even Jo never gave the Brigadier an excuse to say 'She's got hysterics,' as he does at the end of Chapter 17.

When it comes to the Doctor, Hulke makes him rather less abrasive than he appears in 'The Silurians', again perhaps reflecting developments in Jon Pertwee's performance between 1970 and 1973. In one key scene, when he visits Dr Quinn's house, the Doctor of the novelisation is perfectly charming and friendly, quietly hoping to persuade Quinn to confide in him. The equivalent scene on television has the Doctor being deliberately rude and provocative – and getting nowhere. The novel also slightly simplifies the moral ambiguities inherent in Hulke's television scripts, with even the Doctor happily labelling the reptile men 'monsters' on a couple of occasions.

The 'monsters' themselves also gain substantial extra material here. Hulke opens the novel with a prologue, depicting the last hours of reptile dominance on planet Earth, that perhaps could not have been realised on a 1970 television budget. He then takes a few brief camera shots from a Silurian's point of view in Episode 2 and turns them into an entire chapter as seen by one of the reptiles. He also gives individual creatures names: Okdel, Morka and K'to's on-screen equivalents are known only as Old Silurian, Young Silurian and Silurian Scientist. (A later television story, 'Warriors of the Deep', gives the Scientist a different name, Ichtar.)

Terrance Dicks's introduction to this edition alludes to the question of what this race of reptile men should actually be called. They are consistently described as Silurians throughout their eponymous television debut in 1970. A couple of years later, Hulke devised their marine cousins for 'The Sea Devils', giving the Doctor some dialogue (incorrectly) explaining that Silurians was a misnomer and they should have been called Eocenes. By 1974, Hulke had clearly given up on getting the name right, and this novel sticks to 'reptile men' throughout. 'Silurians' makes just one brief appearance, as a password for getting into the research centre. He does, though, have one last stab at accuracy in Chapter 14, with the Doctor suggesting *homo reptilia*.

While *reptile sapiens* might have been more apt, the lasting impact of these Target novelisations was clearly demonstrated almost forty years later, when Matt Smith's Eleventh Doctor encountered a new tribe of reptile men in the 2010 episodes 'The Hungry Earth' and 'Cold Blood'. Describing events previously seen only in this novelisation's prologue, the Doctor says:

> *They're not aliens! They're... Earth-liens! Once known as the Silurian race or, some would argue, Eocenes, or homo reptilia.*

Here are details of other exciting Doctor Who *titles from BBC Books:*

DOCTOR WHO AND THE DALEKS
David Whitaker £4.99
ISBN 978 1 849 90195 6 **A First Doctor adventure**

With a new introduction by **NEIL GAIMAN**

'The voice was all on one level, without any expression at all, a dull monotone that still managed to convey a terrible sense of evil...'

The mysterious Doctor and his granddaughter Susan are joined by unwilling adventurers Ian Chesterton and Barbara Wright in an epic struggle for survival on an alien planet.

In a vast metal city they discover the survivors of a terrible nuclear war – the Daleks. Held captive in the deepest levels of the city, can the Doctor and his new companions stop the Daleks' plan to totally exterminate their mortal enemies, the peace-loving Thals? More importantly, even if they can escape from the Daleks, will Ian and Barbara ever see their home planet Earth again?

This novel is based on the second Doctor Who *story, which was originally broadcast from 21 December 1963 to 1 February 1964. This was the first ever* Doctor Who *novel, first published in 1964.*

DOCTOR WHO AND THE CRUSADERS
David Whitaker £4.99
ISBN 978 1 849 90190 1 **A First Doctor adventure**

With a new introduction by **CHARLIE HIGSON**

'I admire bravery, sir. And bravery and courage are clearly in you in full measure. Unfortunately, you have no brains at all. I despise fools.'

Arriving in the Holy Land in the middle of the Third Crusade, the Doctor and his companions run straight into trouble. The Doctor and Vicki befriend Richard the Lionheart, but must survive the cut-throat politics of the English court. Even with the king on their side, they find they have made powerful enemies.

Looking for Barbara, Ian is ambushed – staked out in the sand and daubed with honey so that the ants will eat him. With Ian unable to help, Barbara is captured by the cruel warlord El Akir. Even if Ian escapes and rescues her, will they ever see the Doctor, Vicki and the TARDIS again?

This novel is based on a Doctor Who *story which was originally broadcast from 27 March to 17 April 1965, featuring the First Doctor as played by William Hartnell, and his companions Ian, Barbara and Vicki.*

DOCTOR WHO AND THE CYBERMEN
Gerry Davis $4.99
ISBN 978 1 849 90191 8 **A Second Doctor adventure**

With a new introduction by **GARETH ROBERTS**

'There are some corners of the universe which have bred the most terrible things. Things which are against everything we have ever believed in. They must be fought. To the death.'

In 2070, the Earth's weather is controlled from a base on the moon. But when the Doctor and his friends arrive, all is not well. They discover unexplained drops of air pressure, minor problems with the weather control systems, and an outbreak of a mysterious plague.

With Jamie injured, and members of the crew going missing, the Doctor realises that the moonbase is under attack. Some malevolent force is infecting the crew and sabotaging the systems as a prelude to an invasion of Earth. And the Doctor thinks he knows who is behind it: the Cybermen.

This novel is based on 'The Moonbase', a Doctor Who story which was originally broadcast from 11 February to 4 March 1967, featuring the Second Doctor as played by Patrick Troughton, and his companions Polly, Ben and Jamie.

DOCTOR WHO AND THE ABOMINABLE SNOWMEN

Terrance Dicks £4.99

ISBN 978 1 849 90192 5 **A Second Doctor adventure**

With a new introduction by **STEPHEN BAXTER**

'Light flooded into the tunnel, silhouetting the enormous shaggy figure in the cave mouth. With a blood-curdling roar, claws outstretched, it bore down on Jamie.'

The Doctor has been to Det-Sen Monastery before, and expects the welcome of a lifetime. But the monastery is a very different place from when the Doctor last came. Fearing an attack at any moment by the legendary Yeti, the monks are prepared to defend themselves, and see the Doctor as a threat.

The Doctor and his friends join forces with Travers, an English explorer out to prove the existence of the elusive abominable snowmen. But they soon discover that these Yeti are not the timid animals that Travers seeks. They are the unstoppable servants of an alien Intelligence.

This novel is based on a Doctor Who *story which was originally broadcast from 30 September to 4 November 1967, featuring the Second Doctor as played by Patrick Troughton, and his companions Jamie and Victoria.*

DOCTOR WHO AND THE AUTON INVASION

Terrance Dicks £4.99
ISBN 978 1 849 90193 2 **A Third Doctor adventure**

With a new introduction by **RUSSELL T DAVIES**

'Here at UNIT we deal with the odd – the unexplained. We're prepared to tackle anything on Earth. Or even from beyond the Earth, if necessary.'

Put on trial by the Time Lords, and found guilty of interfering in the affairs of other worlds, the Doctor is exiled to Earth in the 20th century, his appearance once again changed. His arrival coincides with a meteorite shower. But these are no ordinary meteorites.

The Nestene Consciousness has begun its first attempt to invade Earth using killer Autons and deadly shop window dummies. Only the Doctor and UNIT can stop the attack. But the Doctor is recovering in hospital, and his old friend the Brigadier doesn't even recognise him. Can the Doctor recover and win UNIT's trust before the invasion begins?

This novel is based on 'Spearhead from Space', a Doctor Who story which was originally broadcast from 3 to 24 January 1970, featuring the Third Doctor as played by Jon Pertwee, with his companion Liz Shaw and the UNIT organisation commanded by Brigadier Lethbridge-Stewart.